END OF THE
CYBER DRAGONS

C. T. PHIPPS

&

MICHAEL SUTTKUS

The katana swung at my head before I managed to block it with my own. "Not nearly fast enough, Aiyumi!"

I was wearing a tank top and a pair of athletic shorts as I held the carbon steel blade in my hands while circling around my similarly dressed opponent. I had some height and reach on my opponent, but Aiyumi was quicker and, to be honest, flat out better than me when it came to the martial arts thing.

Aiyumi was pure Japanese, unlike me, in more ways than one. I'd grown up an American refugee and was thoroughly Anglicized despite the fact I'd been raised by my otaku nutjob of a mentor, Snake. Aiyumi, by contrast, had grown up in Japan before undergoing the same crazy person's training.

He'd left more than physical scars on us both and that was why the two of us were presently swinging giant razor blades at each other. The two of us were locked in a concrete room underneath the ground and everything but the clang of blades was blocked out. Only one of us is going to emerge victorious. I was determined it was going to be me, goddammit, because it had to happen eventually.

"You're not supposed to exchange sword blows like a movie, Kei," Aiyumi responded. "Katana are meant to be used as parrying weapons. They're meant to be tools for cutting through hard leathers as well as flesh."

"Oh, was I supposed to wear leather?" I asked, smirking.

FOREWORD

BY C. T. PHIPPS

*W*elcome, fellow cyberpunks!

Revenge of the Cyber Dragons was a great novel that I very much enjoyed writing. Poor Kei never seems to have any end to her problems. No matter how hard she tries to do the right thing, the world always seems to push back hard. In the case of that book, our heroine found herself completely fooled by her ex-teacher and part of a plot that resulted in him helping the cabal that took over the United States.

Despite how enjoyable it's been writing this series, this will be the last of the Cyber Dragons trilogy. First, because it's a trilogy (it's in the name) and second, because I believe that it's best to explore stories to their conclusion rather than try to artificially drag them out. Whether this means that Kei or other members of the party will suffer a horrific fate or not is up to you readers to find out.

Part of what I've enjoyed most about these books is the fact that we've managed to see such intense development with Kei, who has gone from being a Rider trying to make ends meet to an adoptive mother to someone that is now struggling to find her place in the world. I've also enjoyed the character arcs of Paradise, Case, and others.

Creating the world of Cyber Dragons has been a real fun treat as I got to imagine a world of amazing technology, shocking wealth disparity, and ruthless criminals. It was never meant to be social satire, or at least not primarily, but a setting for wild and zany heist adventures. However, I do think I got to comment on what I think are some interesting concepts. We're far off from actual sentient AI, but I think the possibilities are interesting. Things like RealDream, companion machines, and the difference between machine and human consciousness.

Kei is a great character and one that I am going to be sorry to say goodbye to. She's only ever wanted to escape the trauma of her past and it just has a nasty habit of coming back to bite her, no matter how hard she tries to get away. She's also added a nice, working-class perspective on the godlike technology, insidious billionaires, and crazy ninjas that have populated this story.

Those interested in this story and the world involved should note that the Cyber Dragons Trilogy is part of a much larger series of science fiction novels. These include the Agent G books (*Infiltrator*, *Saboteur*, and *Assassin*). These serve as unofficial prequels to the Cyber Dragon Trilogy with the adventures of Case before he met Kei, as well as how the Eruption and the Long Winter played out in our heroes' backstories. Those wanting to see what happens to cyberpunk Earth after the events of this trilogy should check out Moon Cops, Space Academy, and *Lucifer's Star*. This is what I term to be my Futurepunk universe.

Thanks for reading! Please leave a rating or review afterward if you have the time!

CAST OF CHARACTERS

Lead
Keiko "Kei" Springs: Our (anti)heroine. Rider. Ex-Trikuza assassin. Recovering Lethe addict. All-round nice girl. Supposedly.

Supporting
Diane Alders: President of the United States after a *coup d'état*. She is the co-conspirator of Snake and a warhawk.

Patricia "Trish" Ares: A genius created from the fusion of a bioroid and Cognition AI. She is formerly Rebecca Ashe, Kei's daughter, and trying her best to reconcile herself to her new existence. She is the founder of Ares Electronics.

Winston Billions: An exceptionally famous weatherman and comedian who (apparently) dabbles in organized crime. Possibly Kei's little brother, Ken.

Lucita Biondi: A beautiful Italian assassin turned executive. She is a Shell and can throw small cars. Trans. Has a tiny, tiny good side that she denies exists.

Tom Fisher: A cop turned private investigator that is working for the Morrigans.

Barbara Gordon: The chief designer and co-investor in Ares Electronics. She is also Case's daughter.

Case Gordon: Formerly known as "G" and an international man of mystery. Bioroid. Affably evil or evilly affable. Maybe just a cheerful amoral neutral.

Harrison: A bioroid sheep and therapy animal. He's smarter than most of the cast.

Ms. Jones: A Secret Servicewoman intensely loyal to Diane Alders and suspicious of her association with Snake.

Snake Juarez: Trikuza boss. Master assassin. Surrogate dad of Kei and Fate. Seems to be under the impression he's a ninja master and enlightened spiritual killer. Also, not Japanese in the slightest.

Lady of Tigers: One of the four Elemental Lords of the Trikuza and the most traditionalist of the executives. She runs most of their legitimate businesses and is the Chairwoman of the Lightning Tigers.

Neon Rat: One of the four Elemental Lords of the Trikuza and the leader of their seediest businesses like human trafficking, sweat shops, and forced prostitution. He doesn't have a clan to rule over.

Evie Principle: Owner of the This is Paradise brothel and safehouse. Former political activist and revolutionary. Mostly fabulous. Died and was reborn as an all-powerful AI.

Paradise Principle: Evie Principle's daughter. Rider. Way too naive for her job. Supposedly. Raised by the media.

Parvati Rao: A former US Magistrate and Case's ex-girlfriend who made the mistake of trying to do the right thing.

Samantha Sanders: Chairwoman and CEO of Atlas Security. She's a bioroid and former assassin like Case. She's also his ex-wife. Oh, and the mother of the President.

Storm King: One of the four Elemental Lords of the Trikuza and leader of the Steel Phoenixes. The Storm King is one of the most progressive in terms of expanding in fraud, gambling, and loan businesses.

Sun: Lead singer of QuantumCrab and an incredibly powerful Cognition AI. She is internationally famous and releases all her music on infospace. Heavily involved in charities and Third Age spirituality.

Tanaguchi Motoko: The Lady of Tigers' bodyguard and believed lover. He doesn't say much and yet is one of the deadliest men in Japan. He is, unknown to most, Yakuza royalty.

Tanaka Aiyumi: Snake's prize pupil after the loss of Kei and Fate. She is a trained ninja and the daughter of actual Yakuza.

Tanaka Akio: Aiyumi's father and a failed Yakuza gangster. He is currently one of Snake's employees.

Tanaka Hana: Aiyumi's mother and a Yakuza wife. She sold Aiyumi to Snake for membership in the Trikuza for her husband.

Suzuki "Tatski" Tatsuki: A fellow ninja and student of Snake that works for the Trikuza. She is a longtime friend of Aiyumi.

David Yagami: Paradise's boyfriend and Kei's ex. Formerly a police drone operator. Nicer than anyone should be in a cyberpunk dystopia. Theoretically.

CHAPTER ONE

PARADISE LOST, REGAINED, AND LOST AGAIN

The katana swung at my head before I managed to block it with my own. "Not nearly fast enough, Aiyumi!"

I was wearing a tank top and a pair of athletic shorts as I held the carbon steel blade in my hands while circling around my similarly dressed opponent. I had some height and reach on my opponent, but Aiyumi was quicker and, to be honest, flat out better than me when it came to the martial arts thing.

Aiyumi was pure Japanese, unlike me, in more ways than one. I'd grown up an American refugee and was thoroughly Anglicized despite the fact I'd been raised by my otaku nutjob of a mentor, Snake. Aiyumi, by contrast, had grown up in Japan before undergoing the same crazy person's training.

He'd left more than physical scars on us both and that was why the two of us were presently swinging giant razor blades at each other. The two of us were locked in a concrete room underneath the ground and everything but the clang of blades was blocked out. Only one of us is going to emerge victorious. I was determined it was going to be me, goddammit, because it had to happen eventually.

"You're not supposed to exchange sword blows like a movie, Kei," Aiyumi responded. "Katana are meant to be used as parrying weapons. They're meant to be tools for cutting through hard leathers as well as flesh."

"Oh, was I supposed to wear leather?" I asked, smirking.

Aiyumi rolled her eyes and assumed another perfect fighting stance. "Leave the innuendo to Paradise, Kei."

"She's not into innuendo," I replied, trying to stay mobile. "Paradise is more the master of the single entendre."

Paradise was another member of our little group and an ex-prostitute turned dataslicer and Runner. Her mother had been killed by Snake and that had left her in charge of the Morrigans, the world's toughest sex workers union. Strangely, she managed to run it all from our headquarters and it provided what little security we had here.

"She is very social," Aiyumi said. "I am learning much from her."

I raised an eyebrow.

"Sadly, no," Aiyumi said, reminding me that my ninja sparring partner was a lesbian and Paradise was mostly straight. Aiyumi was still a virgin as far as I knew, having been isolated from anyone but Snake since adolescence and he at least had the decency to not take advantage of his students that way. It was about the only decent thing about him. "Focus on your sword fighting, Kei. The old masters could strike down an opponent with one blow."

"Yeah, well, the old master's katanas were made of poor steel and not carbon fiber nanotube so I have an advantage over them," I said, looking for an opening in her defenses. "Also, the ones we're going to use against Snake will have to be able to cut through steel as well as synth flesh."

It was weird having Aiyumi as what amounted to a little sister. I'd had a brother, Ken, who was either dead, alive, or possibly transformed into a cybernetic assassin at Snake's hands. I'd also had Fate, but our relationship had been anything but sisterly. Aiyumi and I were synchronous, though, with so much in common that I really treasured the time we were spending together. Even if I was almost always getting my ass kicked.

"Yes, assuming we ever get the chance," Aiyumi muttered before slipping under my defenses, kicking me in the chest then ducking to sweep me under the leg. I ended up falling on the ground with my sword sliding out of my hand. Aiyumi proceeded to bury the katana into the floor beside my head to emphasize the completeness of her victory.

"Yeah, let's call that one a draw," I said, sighing.

Aiyumi rolled her eyes and extended her hand down to me. "You have improved markedly since we began our training together."

"You think so?" I asked, taking her hand and getting up.

"No," Aiyumi said, dryly. She had a sense of humor; it was just buried deep and tended to be on the sarcastic side. "You have let your *kenjutsu* skills atrophy."

I looked at her, confused. "That just means sword fighting in Japanese. Why mix up your languages?"

Aiyumi frowned. "That is because Snake always said that it was better to do so when dealing with mixed company. It added a sense of, I dunno, cool, in his opinion."

I pinched the bridge of my nose. "Aiyumi, that is because Snake is what we call in the West a weeb. He's a crazy Japanophile that was born in Mexico, trained in Italy, and parties like it's Shogunate Japan. He's not someone you should look up to for how to live your life. The guy knows less about cool than your typical anime nerd and look where it's got him."

"Billions of credits and the title of World's Most Dangerous Man?" Aiyumi said, frowning.

Alright, she had a point there. Still, Aiyumi didn't look happy about having made it. Aiyumi was about twenty but had never lived anything approaching a normal life. I'd managed to escape Snake's control and gotten to live, well, not a normal life but the life of a person. Sex, drugs, rock and roll as well as bills. You know, a life. Aiyumi hadn't even had the chance to live what I had experienced before Snake had killed my parents and pseudo-adopted me. She'd been born to a pair of Trikuza parents who had turned her over to Snake's care from the time she could walk until, well, last year when he'd abandoned her at Elysium.

It had taken a few weeks to begin the cult deprogramming but the fact he'd been willing to discard her like so much trash had left a powerful impression on my pseudo-sister. So had the fact that Snake could have tracked her down if he wanted to. He was now the chief security officer of Atlas Security, the world's largest private army, and the chief hatchet man for the newly elected President of the United States, Diane Alders. We were lying low, but not that low. The fact that he'd so far ignored us was almost... insulting.

"Do you want to be like Snake?" I asked, covered in sweat and wishing the cybernetic enhancements I had didn't include that feature.

"No," Aiyumi said, painfully. "I do not. I wish to be like you, with a family."

I grimaced at Aiyumi's description of my life while struggling to ascertain why it still felt so wrong to say it. I did have a family. I had a daughter in Rebecca, sorry, *Patricia* now. I'd been with Case for the better part of a year and that was longer than any relationship I'd had other than with Fate. Hell, Paradise and Aiyumi were the siblings I'd longed for since Ken's disappearance. So why couldn't I just accept it? Perhaps because I knew what it was like to have it all taken away from you at once. It had happened to me twice.

"Yeah," I said, realizing I'd been standing there with a stupid look on my face for ten seconds. "Family."

"Perhaps we should spar with our fists next," Aiyumi replied, raising hers. "We can also practice our grapples."

I frowned. "Not that the opportunity to get tossed around like a ragdoll isn't appealing but I think our best advantage against Snake will probably involve less hand-to-hand fighting and more a sniper rifle or blowing him up."

Aiyumi frowned. "Killing Snake may be possible, but the consequences are a larger issue. Even I know that."

I gritted my teeth, not at all happy with the situation as she was describing it. Mostly because it was accurate. Snake lived a life as a public figure now and it was possible, we might be able to polish him off (to sound like a comic book). However, that would just bring the entire wrath of Atlas and the United States down upon our heads.

There was also the fact that I was afraid—yes afraid—of going after Snake. He lived rent free in my head and I couldn't drive him out no matter how much I wanted to. I'd tried to. Believe me, I'd tried. Up to and including the fact I'd become a lethe addict for years in hopes of forgetting he ever existed. That had almost killed me.

"Well, we can't just let him go," I muttered, still wrestling with the idea that I wished I could just accept.

"Can't we?" A voice spoke from the training room door.

Paradise was the other younger sibling I'd always wanted but had and lost. Specifically, the annoying Cindy Brady I wanted to give a noogie at all times. Unfortunately, she was fully capable of hacking my cybernetics and causing me to punch myself until I admitted she was the coolest. Not that she'd done that.

Yet.

Paradise Principle, her real name as far as I could tell, was a purple haired South Asian girl who had a tendency to dress in wild and expensive neon clothes that were an assault on the eyes. Her current attire was a Chinese dress with Tron lights and shifting colors that gave me a headache just looking at it. Her hair was tied in the back with lacquered chopsticks, and she was presently holding a datapad that glowed with a holographic interface. Paradise was no older than Aiyumi and yet could do things with computers I could only dream about, and I wasn't a bad hacker myself.

Beside her was David Yagami, a member of our team that I didn't entirely trust anymore. He was a Eurasian boytoy that lent more toward being pretty than traditionally handsome with short black hair and pale smooth skin. David was dressed in a plain white button-down shirt and jeans with a bunch of papers under his arm, which was pretty analog given it was the era of AI as well as cybernetics.

David was formerly a cop and my lover, but he had taken up with Paradise, which were two reasons not to give him the benefit of the doubt. It wasn't jealousy. He'd never been more than a convenience. It was just that he'd decided to bail out of our group after we'd all gotten played by Snake and then had changed his mind a few months later. It was the fact he, a former drone operator at the NLAPD, had tracked us down that told me Snake could have easily done so.

"Can't we what?" I asked, turning to Paradise. "Let them get away with murder?"

"Yeah," Paradise said, nonchalantly. "People get away with it all the time."

It was a distressing attitude because, as much as I hated Snake, Paradise arguably had lost the most between us. Her mother, Evie Principle, had been killed along with a lot of the young men and women who Paradise had grown up with. That Evie had gotten her brain uploaded into being some kind of AI didn't help matters. I couldn't imagine how confusing that would be for most people. Mind you, Paradise wasn't most people.

"Well, *he* shouldn't," I muttered, sounding less confident than I should have been.

It was a stupid statement, and everyone knew it. Three out of four of the people in the room were professional criminals who had gotten away with murder as part of our careers. The fourth was a cop who'd willingly turned a blind eye to it. We'd managed to get out of our last encounter with Snake with our lives, but that was before he'd gotten into the empire building business by aiding in the US coup attempt.

"I support you guys going to kill this guy as long as it doesn't have any blowback on me personally," David said, phrasing it like a joke but clearly as uncomfortable at the prospect of going up against someone as powerful as Atlas Security now as he'd been a year ago.

It wasn't like I blamed him for the attitude. Well, maybe I did a little. A year ago, I'd tried to put aside my past and forge a new life. I'd adopted Rebecca—dammit, Patricia, I needed to remember she'd changed her name—and tried to live a life free from crime. Snake had come to my home and forced himself back into my world.

I'd do one final mission for him, and he'd be out of my life forever. That should have been the end of it. Except, that one final mission had ended up making me an accessory to a terrorist attack and false flag operation that had ended up putting Diane Alders in the Oval Office. The US government had been involved in three wars since then, most of them ending in occupations of much-smaller nations and the body count was in the low millions. A fourth war was already in the works, and no one seemed inclined to stop her.

"Perhaps we should take a break," Aiyumi muttered, picking

up on the helplessness mixed with my rage. Two qualities that only fed one another.

"Yeah," I said, walking over to my bag beside the training area and picking up my towel to wipe off the sweat on my face. "Actually, no, I think I'm done for today. Do you mind cleaning up?"

Aiyumi frowned. "Certainly."

Paradise looked at me and put her arms on my side. "Hey, did you not think I might have a reason for coming down here?"

"Yeah," David said, supporting her in that David-esque way he did things. Which was as noncommittally as possible.

"Which is?" I asked, not really caring that much.

"We're getting married," Paradise said, lifting her hand with a ring.

I stared. "Uh huh."

"Paradise picked out the ring," David said, cheerfully.

"I assume she paid for it too," I muttered.

Aiyumi, who was now at my side, gave me an elbow to the ribs.

"Congratulations!" I said, faking as much sincerity as I could, which admittedly, wasn't much. "It's a big step."

It was also a horrific mistake, but I had yet to encounter any friend, good or otherwise, who appreciated being told when they were making one. However, I suspected this wasn't just her making an announcement for her sake. Paradise, despite her somewhat goofy demeanor, never did anything without a reason.

"Yeah, I thought it was time to move on with my life," Paradise said, her tone letting me know exactly what she was really after.

"Ah," I said, sighing. "Good for you."

It wasn't just enough that Paradise disagreed with my decision to keep focus on ways we might eventually strike at Snake. No, she was using her upcoming nuptials as a way to try and stage an intervention. An intervention I neither wanted nor needed.

I wasn't the crazy one, was I? Snake was the one who had ruined my life and the lives of so many other people. Yes, he was rich and powerful now. Well, he'd always been rich and powerful, but now he was super-rich and powerful. Anyway, that didn't mean he was beyond justice, did it? Hell, even revenge. I didn't care about the difference between the two. Were we just supposed to throw our hands up in the air, go "Oh well, I guess that's that", and pretend nothing had happened?

Except, honestly, I suspected that was exactly what they were expecting me to do. Even Aiyumi, the only other person that I believed understood just how deep Snake's violation had gone, was hesitant to do any active work against him. I liked to think it was just because she understood how dangerous he was, but another part of me believed it was that everyone else had already given up. Well fine, then, I'd do it myself.

"So would you like to be the best woman?" Paradise asked.

"Excuse me?" I asked, shaken from my thoughts.

"Matron of Honor," David corrected.

"Whatever," Paradise said, shrugging. "This is all just a magical ritual where we beseech the blessings of the gods anyway. So, like, do we sacrifice a goat or what?"

David's eyes widened.

"It's also a legal contract," Aiyumi pointed out.

"Yeah, but I'm a professional criminal who refuses to be bound by the petty laws of mere mortals," Paradise said, without a trace of irony. "Would they accept a pigeon? Because there's a bunch of pigeons outside. I can afford a goat but they're cute and pigeons are the dirty hobos of the sky."

"They used to be popular pets," David said, smiling.

"Shut up, no one cares," Paradise said, snapping at David.

David just smiled and made a locking gesture with his fingers around his mouth. If nothing else, I suspected the marriage would be comfortable with who was in charge.

I was tempted just to flat out refuse, say, "Well, I'll see if I can fit it in my schedule when I'm not plotting to kill the second most powerful person in America." However, I wasn't angry at Paradise. Not that much. I was angry at Snake and myself. Angry at the situation.

"Sure!" I said, through clenched teeth. "Absolutely! Sounds super."

Okay, that could have been slightly more convincing. I could have maybe had a big sweater on that said, I AM A LIAR.

Neither Paradise nor David looked impressed.

Before I could try to salvage the situation, I heard another voice speak nearby. Turning once more to the door, I saw a white fleece sheep who was wearing a pair of glasses and a fedora. It was Harrison (Ford), our electric sheep. "Hello, Kei."

"What is it, Harrison?" I asked, not too politely. Unfortunately, I'd come to resent Harrison as well. It was hard to be angry and furious when you had something so adorable around you all the time.

"Case wants to speak with you," Harrison said.

I looked down at the ring on my finger, still unsure about why I'd agreed to it as well. "Let's go see what my husband has to say."

CHAPTER TWO

SEATTLE IS ITS OWN STATE

Married.

Me.

Yeah, I bet y'all didn't see that coming? I know I didn't. It just sort of happened when I was trying to get my new life set up here in Seattle. I was still rocking from the transformations to Becky—dammit, Patricia—and Case suggested we do it. We'd had a small ceremony, gotten hitched, and pretty much went back to the exact same routine we'd had beforehand.

Still, it was a weird sensation and one I wasn't entirely comfortable with. My longest lasting relationship beforehand had been with Fate and that had ended with her betraying me. Well, it had ended when I'd split her in half with a thermal katana, but it was still not exactly a good sign that I was prepared for marriage. A part of me was certain I was going to screw this up and it bothered me that I was concerned about that when I was plotting to go to war with Snake as well as Atlas Security.

I mean, prioritize, Kei.

I was thinking all of this as I headed down the hall and stepped into an elevator to take me up when I heard a small British-accented voice. "Hold the elevator, would you?"

My attention darted down to the three-foot-tall sheep wearing a tie and sporting an Indiana Jones-style fedora. He walked into the elevator and took up a position next to me. The incongruous and adorable creature was Case's majordomo and my daughter's most frequent babysitter, Harrison. Technically, he was Harrison II as the original had sacrificed his life to try to take down the Elysium murder hotel. Except, he was an AI, so he had a backup and had basically just resumed life as before.

That was another thing I was trying to deal with: my increasing association with all this crazy transhumanist-post-human AI crap. Was I supposed to treat Harrison as back from the dead, cloned, or just the exact same artificial sheep-bot that he's always been? What about Patricia? Was she still Becky, the girl I'd adopted, or some new sort of person walking around in a new body? She'd been an adolescent before and now she was wearing the Jennifer Lawrence-looking body of an adult woman. I'd talk to Case about it, but he was a bioroid himself and I wasn't sure if he could understand all my concerns or would just think I was being racist?

Robotocist?

Robophobic?

Dammit.

"So, still adjusting to your new circumstances, Kei?" Harrison asked as the doors shut on us.

"Wait, what?" I asked, doing a double take at the sheep.

"I have specialized sensors that can detect your stress and emotional difficulties," Harrison said.

"You do?" I asked, surprised.

"Yes, they're called eyes," Harrison said, demonstrating that everyone in this place was a wiseass.

"Funny," I muttered, pushing the button for the Ares Electronics offices. It occupied the top ten floors of the building except for the penthouse.

The choice to move out of the New Los Angeles (finally called "New Angeles" by people who were sick of three names) arcology and to the still-rebuilding city of Seattle had been one I'd questioned. After all, if the US government (considered a joke since the Eruption and eager to make up for lost time) wanted to drone strike us then it wasn't like they couldn't find us here anymore than in NLA.

Still, I was becoming used to the Persephone Building. It was a weirdly named acquisition by Case's holding company. The office building had been abandoned during the Eruption and had been refurbished when most people would have just demolished it to put up a super skyscraper as was the way these days. It was weirdly homey as a result and pretty much every-one lived as well as worked within its confines. Still, every time I looked outside the windows, I couldn't help but feel it was less like my home and more like my cage.

My mind was full of these kinds of cheerful thoughts as the elevator started rising through the floors of the century-old structure.

"It's not meant to be funny," Harrison said, standing there pensive. "I remind you that I'm designed as a therapy animal."

"Case's daughter made you to be his butler," I said, correcting him. "Not any sort of therapist."

"Companion," Harrison said, pausing. "Either way, I can tell you're hurting, Kei, and I wanted to be the one to reach out."

The sheer ridiculousness of the scene was something that prevented me from feeling genuinely touched. After all, it wasn't like I'd had many friends in my childhood and the ones I'd made here were equally screwed up. Most of my current companions, I suspected, were trying to give me space and that was the worst thing to give me right now. Except, I couldn't be the one to reach out and say so. No, the only person who was actually trying was a robot sheep.

"It's complicated, Harrison," I replied.

"Your teacher and surrogate father for most of your devel-oping life betrayed you and used you as a weapon to kill thou-sands of people," Harrison said. "But it's been almost a year, and everyone seems in no hurry to pick a fight with him. Most likely because doing so will almost certainly lead to the death of everyone involved."

I blinked. "Yeah, basically, that."

"The Sicilian concept of the vendetta is one that avenging one's loved ones is a task for which you should be willing to put aside all thought to your personal safety and be willing to die in order to achieve," Harrison said.

"Yeah, when seeking revenge dig two graves," I said, sigh-ing. "I've heard the saying before."

"I've always felt that was a very stupid way to live," Harrison replied. "The cycles of revenge ended up depopulating the populations of whole towns. What is the purpose of revenge if it leaves your loved ones grieving even more?"

"The knowledge that Snake isn't going to hurt anyone else," I said, dryly. "He's starting wars now, you know."

"Alas, the engines of the United States military-industrial complex are far bigger than your old teacher," Harrison said, sighing. "The United States lost a great deal of power and respect when the Yellowstone caldera erupted. It spent decades rebuilding and lost millions of lives in the process."

"I was there, sheep," I said, reminding him. "My parents begged, borrowed, and stole to keep me alive."

And my brother.

Couldn't forget him.

One of the mind games Snake had done to me was to tell me my brother, Ken, was still alive. That he'd survived the murder of our parents and been inducted into the Trikuza. Winston Billions, the assassin who enjoyed using drone bodies to carry out his murders, had claimed to be him. Snake had claimed to be him, but I had no way of verifying whether that was the truth since they were both liars.

"What I am saying is that it is now the American empire's desire to rebuild the respect and fear they once wielded on the international stage," Harrison said. "Diane Alders has the support of most of the nation to restore the Pax Americana. Snake, being a Mexican ninja, is only interested in how he can profit from it."

The President of the United States was someone that Case apparently knew. The adopted daughter of Atlas Security's Chairwoman, Samantha Sanders, she'd grown up at the foot of the world's largest private military and arms manufacturer. I'd wanted to know more about his connection but, husband or not, Case had been surprisingly quiet on the subject. It made me wonder if he was afraid I was going to go utterly nuts and try and go Lee Harvey Oswald on her.

No. I wasn't.

As reprehensible as I currently found the unelected POTUS, I wasn't stupid. Taking out Snake and surviving the subsequent retaliation was just barely possible. Taking out the head of state? Especially as she was riding high from her victories in Southeast Asia? Not a chance. Besides, I didn't want to start a civil war. As much as I wanted revenge against everyone who'd used me as a pawn at Elysium, I wasn't about to drag the rest of the country into my crap.

"None of that helps me," I said, firmly, wishing this elevator ride was over. "I'm not even sure what you're trying to say."

"I'm saying maybe you should consider that this is a long struggle for justice," Harrison said. "One that may take years or even decades for Snake to have an opening that you might be willing or able to exploit."

"Life is what happens when you're busy making other plans," I said, quoting John Lennon. "Here's the thing, though, I can't."

"You can't what?" Harrison asked, looking up at the numbers we were passing. The Persephone building wasn't as tall as the Columbia Center but was close. It used to be called the Washington Mutual Tower and had fifty-five stories. We were about thirty up now. I was still getting used to the idea of private elevators that people like me could use without ever having to deal with the "little people." People I already missed being able to deal with.

"Live," I said, surprising myself by having a little bit of a breakthrough with that statement. "I'm not a businesswoman, Harrison. I'm not a housewife or kept woman. I'm a street merc. I used to deliver packages, smuggle goods, and shoot people. That was my job, that was who I am. I made a game effort to be Becky's mom, but now? Well, she's an adult. Sort of."

"I see," Harrison observed.

"Do you?" I asked. "Or am I baring my soul to a talking animal that's probably copyrighted by the Disney Corporation."

"Heaven forbid," Harrison said, offended at the prospect of being a Disney product. "You're bored."

I crossed my arms. "It's a bit more complicated than that."

"Is it?" Harrison asked. "Idle hands are the Devil's workshop."

"We're not doing a competition on the old timey sayings we can quote," I replied. "At least I think we aren't."

"Then don't bring up Lennon," Harrison retorted. "It's bad enough that you know Snake got away with using you to kill a large number of innocent people. However, you've had clients do that before at the DataSecure heist. It took a while for that to happen, though. No, the problem is you have nothing to occupy your mind but revenge. So, it's just festering in your mind."

"It's not that simple," I said, feeling defeated.

"Sure, it is," Harrison said. "We just need to find you something to do."

I didn't bring up that I hadn't been able to deal with the fact that Fate once used me to kill innocent people in the same way Snake had used me at Elysium. At DataSecure, she'd made me part of a bombing designed to cover up our theft of the Sun AI fragments. Those deaths had been in the hundreds. At Elysium, Snake had used me as a vector that uploaded a rage-virus that had turned the hotel's staff into a bunch of murder-crazed zombies. Ones that were worse than the ones in movies because they'd kept their ability to use weapons.

What Harrison seemed to be ignoring was that I'd spent years trying to forget what had happened with Fate and had turned to, let's just say, *pharmaceutical* methods of dealing with the pain. Lethe was a euphoric drug that had the very distinctive ability of erasing only your worst memories, the ones that caused you pain. The thing was that I'd had so much trauma linked to Snake and Fate that it had carved out whole chunks of my past. It had been killing me toward the end, but I'd been able to move on.

Or so I thought.

I didn't want to admit it but Sun restoring all my memories and all of the expensive treatments I never would have been able to afford to keep me alive were things I sometimes considered just throwing away. The physiological addiction to lethe was gone from my body but not the psychological one. If I never took another dose, I'd still live to a maximum of another fifty years thanks to the damage it had done to my brain, but if I got myself using again then I would end up dead in twenty for sure. That seemed like a long time to me but with cybernetics, people were already predicting the rich would last two hundred or more years. But what was the point of that if you hated your life? And why did I feel so guilty for hating it when everyone was trying to make me happy?

"Yeah," I said, realizing I needed to respond to Harrison's suggestion. "That sounds great."

With that, the elevator pinged and opened its doors to the extremely busy interior of Ares Electronics. It was a tech start up when virtually every other tech company in the world was owned and operated by one of the preexisting megacorporations.

The company had been founded by Patricia Ares—it seemed that she didn't want to use my last name anymore, either—and Barbara Gordon merging their respective ideas into one single corporate vision. Combined with Case's millions and the bribe money Snake had so generously slipped into all of our accounts, it was taking off as a company manufacturing bioroid parts alongside AI supplements. I had no idea what half of the stuff they did was for and, honestly, didn't understand the jargon itself.

That was another thing that was bothering me that I didn't know how to reconnect with Becky. She had been dying due to Snake's secret modifications of her brain and the only way to save her had been to "upgrade" her with a gift from Sun the AI. Except, I barely recognized Becky right now. She'd gone from being a girl interested in boy bands and the latest season of *Married in 30 Days*. Now she was calculating the kind of fuel payload necessary to get up a communications satellite without bumping into other space junk.

The interior of the office building was full of the largest collection of hackers, dataslicers, techjacks, and cyberpunks I'd seen outside of a QuantumCrab concert. They weren't all behind cubicles, but they all had their own workstations as a bunch of holographic monitors were displaying massive amounts of ticking numbers that I had no idea how to decipher. The walls were decorated in band posters, the floors in bean bags, and there was a very DIY feel to the place.

Seattle had been home to a lot of anarchist collectivists as well as people unwilling to trust the government in the aftermath of the Long Winter. Somehow, Case had recruited a huge chunk of people who were generally anti-corporate and antiso-cial before putting them to work making whatever it was that Ares Electronics did.

"Patricia asked about you," Harrison said, walking with me into the office. "She says you've been avoiding her. Again."

"Yeah, I can't imagine why," I muttered.

"As an artificial life form, I know something about going through monumental changes," Harrison said. "I can advise you that she's still the same person that she was before."

"I know," I said, lying.

"I just think you should go speak with her," Harrison said.

"I'll make time," I said, lying as I headed up to Case's office. It occurred to me that I was going up to him like he was my boss rather than my husband and I decided to give him the business about that.

We'd had a good six months together before things had started to fall apart, which was admittedly just this last month. He'd tried very hard to console me, give me all the attention and love I'd needed but it wasn't enough. Snake needed to die so that I could live. That was the line I was drawing in the sand.

I tried not to think about the fact that if this didn't work, if I was still empty after Snake died, that I'd have nothing at all to motivate me. I had that in my mind when I entered Case's office with its view of the Seattle skyline. He was standing in front of a window, looking pensive and talking to a white suited man with their back turned.

"There is a reason you couldn't come personally?" I asked, annoyed.

That was when the other man in the room turned around and I saw the face of Winston Billions.

My so-called brother.

I launched myself at his throat.

CHAPTER THREE

ENEMY OF MY ENEMY

Winston.
Ken.

Frick, I didn't know which was his real name or whether the son of a bitch had one. However, the golden-haired and golden-skinned man was a Shell and that meant assaulting him was a bit like assaulting a tank in a human skinsuit. My fists impacted his body, and I felt like I had punched a steel girder covered in foam carpeting.

If I didn't break my knuckles on the initial attack, it was only because of my own enhancements and that wasn't enough to stop me from attempting to knee him in the nuts as well. That, unfortunately, was blocked by his hand. Winston—the name I decided I was going to refer to him as—didn't attack in return. That just infuriated me more.

"Kei!" Case called from the other side of the room.

"Give me a gun!" I shouted, half expecting him to say to stop my attack.

"Okay," Case said, going to his desk and removing an Archangel-19 pistol. "Do you want explosive bullets?"

"Obviously!" I replied.

"Okay," Case said, sliding in a clip. "Do you want me to put a round in the chamber or not?"

Case was obviously stalling to give me a moment to calm down and I had to admit it was an ingenious strategy. It gave me a moment to analyze the fact Winston wasn't attacking and there wasn't an army of ninjas behind him. Why I specifically thought he'd attack with an army of ninja just went to show you what sort of number that Snake had done on my brain.

I pulled back and assumed a defensive stance before Case tossed me the pistol that I turned on Winston. "Don't make a move or you're dead."

I wanted to shoot him.

I really did.

But if I did, I'd probably never find out the truth of whether he was Ken or not. Ironically, that almost got me to shoot him anyway. After all, if I shot him then I never would have it confirmed that my brother became every bit the narcissistic psychopath that Snake was. One that I couldn't even see beneath his artificial body that had removed every trace of my mother's ancestry.

Winston, to his credit, just raised his hands. "I am unarmed, sister."

"Don't call me that!" I said, growling. "Case, what the hell is going on?"

I didn't look at Case, but his face was burned into my brain. My husband with his chiseled features and perpetually shadow-darkened skin. There was an everywhere to his features and yet a nowhere that made him able to impersonate almost anyone from anywhere on Earth. So much so that his most memorable qualities were his Cheshire Cat smile and extreme fashion sense that were worse than useless for identifying him.

"Mr. Billions is here to offer us a deal," Case said. "Believe me, I was less than happy to find him in our office as well. He was lucky I didn't kill him."

"I think you overestimate your remaining skill, bioroid," Winston said with more than a hint of contempt. "You were obsolete when the Long Winter happened and every year, technology just leaves you further and further in the dust."

I stared at him. "You seem to be forgetting where the hell you are. And while I think you can probably beat Case—"

"Rude," Case muttered.

Which, to be fair, Winston was. However, the days when Case was the most cutting-edge murder machine on the market were long gone.

"I'm pretty sure I could finish you off," I said, coldly at him. "Not to mention all the other people in the building who would love to take a shot at you."

Winston looked ready to deliver a snide remark that would have justified my blowing his face off before he caught himself. "I'm not here to make enemies."

"You made enemies of me a long time ago," I said, remembering the assault on Fate's mansion. Winston had supposedly been an ally then, too. "Okay, since he isn't dead, what is this deal he's willing to offer that I'll enjoy more than finishing off this piece of crap?"

Winston had tried to kill me multiple times but the thing that had made me hate him the most was what he'd done to Becky. While I'd been out there, working and struggling to make a life away from organized crime and Running, he'd broken in and kidnapped Becky to turn her into a listening device for his boss. The modifications he'd made were more than a violation and had forced her to undergo the process that had left us so distant. If I wasn't worried that he was my brother, I would have killed him much earlier.

But was that enough for me not to kill him? I wasn't sure anymore. My brother had died as far as I'd known many years ago. Before I'd been separated from my family and gone through all of the insane training I thought had made me Snake's disciple but had really just made me into his tool. It should have been a tearful reunion between us, but the simple fact was, whether he was an imposter or not, all I'd gotten from Winston was misery.

"Such language from a young mother," Winston said, chidingly. He was joking as 'crap' was about as salty as I got with my language.

Okay, now he had to die. "Was good seeing you, Winston. See you again, in hell."

"I want to help you kill Snake," Winston said, his smugness never wavering. Some people were just genetically programmed to be assholes. Which, given he was possibly my brother, wasn't a good sign.

"You have a few seconds to explain," I replied, keeping my gun focused on him.

For now.

"Okay, that was way too easy," I said, standing up.

"We got lucky," Ms. Jones said, standing up.

"No, she's right," Samantha said, already up herself. "That was a distraction. This is all theater, including shooting us down."

"Do you think so?" Lucita asked, one hand holding her info-pad and the other with my Archangel-19. "They hit us with a rocket."

"Did they?" Samantha asked, clearly putting this together in her head. "They could have rigged the limousine instead. Both the computer and a bomb that would look like we'd been hit without actually threatening our lives. Basic Hollywood special effects. Then they send in the gunships to chase us, so it looks like a failed assault that only he could have pulled off, but the gunships were rigged to fail as well. This could all be an attempt to make it look like Snake was trying to kill us."

"Why?" I asked confused.

That was when both Ms. Jones and Samantha aimed their rifles at me. They didn't hold them up at sniper point but at their waists, aimed at my center mass. Which was unnecessary since a shot at close range would cause me to become nothing short of an enormous splatter across the ground.

"Oh, come on!" I said, dropping my rifle and lifting my hands. "You can't believe I'm capable of pulling something like this off."

Lucita stood behind them, looking conflicted.

"I think you underestimate our opinion of you," Samantha said, her voice cold but holding hints of barely held back fury.

"Why would I do it?" I asked, already knowing why she might think this.

"To make sure we supported you against Snake," Samantha replied. "A pity, I think we could have worked well together. Goodbye, Ms. Springs."

That was when Lucita shot Ms. Jones and Samantha Sanders in the back of the head. The sudden action took me by surprise, and I couldn't help but take a step back to stare at the result as Lucita proceeded to shoot both women on the ground, double tapping them in the head to make absolutely sure that they were dead.

"Mother pus bucket," I said, taking a step back and looking at the corpses.

Lucita took a deep breath and tossed the gun back to me. I caught it and briefly wondered about whether she was framing me. Instead, she looked at me. "You should dispose of that weapon. I'm the person most likely to handle this investigation, though, so you don't have to worry about being implicated."

"You just killed the most powerful woman in the world," I said, knowing that she'd both saved my life as well as betrayed her longest ally. Which didn't make sense.

Even if Lucita and I had bonded.

"Yes," Lucita said, her voice losing its accent. "President Alders now will believe that her lover, Snake, killed her mother. It didn't go as well as I'd hoped but it should provide enough of a personal grudge that we can force him to go on the run. Diane may not have always seen eye to eye with her mother, but she did love her. As much as the super-rich are capable of loving, at least."

I stared at her. "Lucita, this can't have—"

"I'm not Lucita," Lucita said, smiling.

It all fell into place.

Frick.

"Winston," I said, aloud.

"I'm still not Ken yet in your mind?" Winston asked with Lucita's face.

CHAPTER TEN
MY FAMILY SUCKS

"Am I not yet Ken, sister?" Winston asked, his voice lowering until it was identical to his normal one. It was a disconcerting sight to see it coming from a friend's mouth and left me feeling unsure how to react.

"What the hell is this?" I asked, looking down at Samantha and Ms. Jones' corpses.

"I thought I explained it pretty well," Winston said, proud of himself, herself, themselves. I was confused.

I took a deep breath. "We were supposed to ally with them."

"Were we?" Winston said, looking down at the bodies. "One thing I learned while in the Trikuza's care is you can't trust anyone. They might have used you to eliminate Snake and then immediately abandoned you to face President Alder's justice."

I couldn't believe this. "Did you set this all up? The rocket? The gunships? We have to leave."

Winston looked annoyed. "Of course, I set all of this up. Do you think I would leave anything to chance? Why do you think I'm wearing Lucita's body?"

A chill ran down my spine. "Is she dead?"

Winston chuckled and gestured for me to follow him. "She's presently in hiding. Of the Atlas Corp board of directors, she has always been the most violently opposed to Snake's position. He was under the impression that I was going to be using the resources I used here to replace her. Which I have, at least for a time. I admit, being a woman doesn't suit me and I'll have to change soon."

I admitted that a part of me was relieved that Lucita was alive. However, I'd clearly been spending too much time around suits, because a part of me had been wondering how Winston had been able to afford a Lucita-style body. Shells cost somewhere to the effect of ten million UN credits or twenty million in new dollars. That was a lot to spend on an assassination.

That is, assuming I believed him, and he wasn't just lying about killing her. He could have stolen her body and substituted either his brain or another drone package. No, he couldn't be a drone this time. The limousine had been blocking all signals and we'd had our feed jammed out here. This had to be the real Winston.

If such a creature existed.

"Does your body really matter to you at this point?" I asked. "Every time I see you, you're in another robot. I would have thought you stopped caring about shapes long ago."

Winston stared, his eyes showing through Lucita's face. "I have a dozen at my beck and call. All of them linked together and plenty of them coordinated doing routines via Dummy AI. Most people can't even tell the difference when talking with them. The guy on the weather? Winston Billions? The real one? That's actually me too. So is a janitor, a face cream model, and a few others. Each of them costs ten million credits a shell. I don't own any of them, but I have to move through them constantly, consciousness wise, because that's what I've been made to do."

"By Snake?" I asked.

"By the experiments," Winston said, closing his—Her? Their? —eyes. It was only a moment, and I was tempted to shoot my supposed brother between the eyes. I'd never be able to pull it off with the rifle, though.

Maybe their chest.

"What experiments?" I asked. "Why did they make you into this?"

"You don't believe I'm your brother, do you?" Winston asked, sounding almost... wistful.

"My brother died. You, if you're a remnant of him at all, aren't my brother. My brother would never abuse my daughter or try to kill me. That's not how family behaves."

Winston's expression was cold, and it was strange seeing it with Lucita's face. "No, Snake or his goons didn't kill me like they killed our parents. The Trikuza isn't that wasteful. Snake has always been a child snatcher and there was always a never-ending source of refugee children to bring into his cult. There still is. I have the memories of dozens."

I blinked, confused. "What?"

"Ken Springs wasn't as lucky as you, Kei," Winston said. "I remember the petty thievery, beatings, starvings, and rapes that he was subjected to. He wasn't the golden child raised in one of Snake's many apartments and turned into a Special Forces assassin. No, he was just another disposable piece of street trash that either learned to survive or died. It was a story I remember from so many perspectives."

"I don't understand," I said, now suddenly getting the impression I was in danger. Which was something I should have felt much earlier.

I could also hear more vehicles coming into the park. The police had finally arrived and so had other parties—we should have left much earlier.

"Ken eventually screwed up," Winston said. "When he was fourteen and already working the streets, he stole from one of his clients. That's not something you do when you're trying to build repeat business as a catamite and his owner cut him badly. So much so that he was useless. That's when Snake found a use for him. To be part of his experiments to create an AI. To join the hivemind he was trying to string together to make his ultimate weapon. It didn't work enough to create a creature like Sun or Eve. But I was born from the dozens of brains in a jar that was all that was left of the Trikuza's broken slaves."

I released a breath I hadn't known I was holding. He wasn't Ken. Maybe he was partially Ken, but he wasn't just Ken. It wasn't Ken's fault what happened to Becky. That action came from some other bit of Winston, some other victim of Snake's plotting. It was a relief that I didn't have to hate family.

Did it really make sense? Should I be relieved? I didn't know. I could think about the details later. Or, more likely, not. Self-analysis had never been my strong suit. The important thing was, I didn't need to feel confused about him. He wasn't my brother. Just... a piece of him? No, that line of thought would lead to more confusion. I needed to stay focused on the here and now. Stick to the simple answers. The ones that released me.

I could kill him without having to face the ghosts of my parents.

Winston lowered the gun in their hand and said, almost like a child, "You're the only family I have left."

He had to go and make this more complicated.

"We need to get out of here," I said. The cops were useful for the first time in my life, saving me from having to think through this right now. "If you want to be part of my family, you're going to have to make amends."

Why the hell had I said that? What was I thinking? I believed Winston now, which was probably a mistake. If his story was a lie—which it almost certainly was—it made sense with what I knew of this strange and surreal situation I'd found myself in. I knew that Snake had long been interested in AI and their potential as weapons. And the Trikuza wasn't a bunch of romantic rogues that would hesitate to turn a bunch of broken-down adolescents into fodder for their experiments.

There was also the fact that even if he was forgivable as a child, he was now irredeemable as an adult. Or was he? I couldn't decide. A tragic past didn't excuse a horrible adulthood, but who was I to judge? I'd been involved in more bloody shootouts and murders than three street gangs. I was married to a former professional assassin of the kind James Bond used to kill. Hell, all the people I knew were monsters except for Paradise.

And that was because judging Paradise for what she did was like judging Bugs Bunny for putting a carrot in a rifle barrel before it blows up someone. Could it be that I wanted to try to save Winston? Could it be that I did? I didn't know and there wasn't a right answer. Especially as he'd just murdered two allies. That was when Winston was shot in the throat, which caught me off guard as much as anything else. The look in their eyes as white fluid started pouring from his throat, followed by a second shot that struck him in the shoulder.

"Dammit!" I said, daring to look over my shoulder and turning to see Aiyumi holding her pistol as Paradise followed behind her. I saw one of the flying cars from the parking garage behind them and guessed they'd boosted it, which was both impressive and stupid. Apparently, they hadn't trusted the President's mother to deal straight with me.

"Move!" Aiyumi shouted, aiming to fire a third shot into the false Lucita.

I froze. I never freeze, but I froze. I wanted Winston dead. I wanted to save him. I wanted to scream at Aiyumi to stop and celebrate her shot at the same time. It had been Snake's first lesson that there was nothing worse to do in a conflict than freeze, but I stood there, trying to decide which way I should move, unable to make myself do anything at all.

But there was only one way to get this wrong that I couldn't walk back. I put myself in front of Aiyumi's next shot. "Stop!"

Aiyumi looked confused at my sudden movement and stood there as Paradise came to a halt beside her.

"What's going on?" Paradise asked, clearly not sure what the hell was going on and I couldn't blame her.

After all, how the hell would I even begin to explain what was going on? There was also the fact the police were about to descend on us. Which, given one of the richest people on Earth had just been killed as well as a member of the President's security detail, I could only assume our situation would involve lots of shooting people who looked like me. I remembered the boathouse and wondered if Winston had planned our escape route to be genuinely through that location or if it had always been a trap.

But right now, my primary concern was whether or not to try to save him or finish him off. God, why the hell did this have to be so complicated? I wasn't even sure if what he'd told me was true or just more lies. What was he even if he was telling the truth? Just some of my brother's memories implanted on a machine running on a server somewhere? Would dying here even kill him or just shut down whatever program he was running here? Was what he said enough to drive me to do something incredibly stupid? Just one moment of vulnerability and he'd gone from being a monster to a person? What did I owe him? If anything?

"Winston, can you run? Do you have an escape route?" Because I certainly didn't have one.

Winston looked a lot worse than I expected as he produced large amounts of white fluid from his injuries and looked like he was debating shooting us all despite it. His voice was stuttering, cracking in a mixture of several different tones. It shifted between Lucita's and his own now. "No, I cannot. There's a route in the boathouse, though. Ironic."

"Yeah," I said, throwing my rifle on the ground and trying to lift him up. "Ironic."

"Wire Paradise to me," Winston said, not helping. "The information is inside me."

"What?" I started to ask. "What—"

"Do it," Winston said. "Then I will delete this instance of my personality. Leave no trace."

Of course, he was just a copy. I kicked myself again.

"Of course," I said. I picked him up. Luckily, I was stronger than I looked. If his escape was through the boathouse, that meant going toward the lake. I turned to my friends. "Come on!"

"Leave this body behind," Winston said, resisting. "And when you next see me, shoot first."

"What?" I asked confused.

"This body contains the last remnants of your brother," Winston said. "Goodbye."

"What? No," I said, immediately panicking.

That was when another bullet struck his back. I turned around and saw a pair of police officers shouting at us while another was shooting. They were, of course, warning us to lay down our weapons as they attempted to gun us down. I'd forgotten how much I hated New Angeles' cops. Protect and serve my toned butt.

"Frick!" I yelled, dropping Winston as I opened fire at the cop who had just shot my brother before ducking behind a tree.

"Hey, why are we staying here and getting shot at?" Paradise asked, also seeking cover. "I mean, I love getting shot at by the cops as much as the next girl, but..."

"Ken left a data file for you," I said, seeing the cops getting their own cover and falling back. Unfortunately, a bunch more were heading our way. "Wire up and get it."

"Sure, I'll just patch my brain to this guy who keeps trying to kill us, why not?" Paradise muttered, running across the ground like a child across a playground.

"Just do it!" I shouted. "Aiyumi and I will keep the cops distracted." With that, I turned to Aiyumi and said, "Not killing them might minimize how hard they chase us later."

Okay, she probably hadn't heard that.

"And it might make them shoot at us harder now!" Aiyumi said, showing she had. She fired repeatedly.

"Well, shoot them harder if they get aggressive!" I said, shooting again.

"Okay, I'm done," Paradise said, getting up and seemingly immune to all bullets. "We're going to have a minute."

"What do you mean—" I started to ask as an ear-piercing horrifying whine filled my ears and caused me to drop my gun. It also seemed to affect Aiyumi—though she kept her gun—as well as all of the cops that were seemingly forming an army. That was when I saw the police cars hovering around suddenly lose power and fall from the sky, crashing about a dozen. I had no idea what Paradise had done but I wasn't about to waste an opportunity. I bolted for the boat house with Aiyumi following behind, the painful whine still in my head.

"Where are we going?" Aiyumi asked.

"Boathouse!" I said.

"Sure! Why didn't I think of that!" Aiyumi said, showing a rare sarcastic side.

It's hard to explain details while you're running, even when your lungs are half polymer. Surprisingly, Paradise moved faster than all of us and arrived at the boat house first. There was a little more gunfire as we reached the door, and I pulled it open.

The interior of the boathouse was pretty much just what you'd expect with a bunch of equipment for the suits to use on their vacations. There was also a pair of motorboats docked in an interior pier, but that wasn't going to help us. I was about to despair when I noticed that there was also a hatch on the ground. I ran to it and pried it open, revealing a ladder leading down a long metal chute.

I turned to the others. "Move!"

That was when I noticed that Aiyumi was bleeding from her back, a mixture of red and white fluid coming from where she'd obviously been shot. Aiyumi's expression was one of agony, but she was staring forward, as if the mission was something that trumped the fact she was seriously injured.

Paradise bolted the door, which would do jack all to deal with the police that were probably seconds behind us.

"Can you climb?" I asked Aiyumi.

"I don't have a choice," Aiyumi said, struggling.

"I could carry you," I said.

"It's a ladder."

"Okay, fair."

I climbed down first and watched Aiyumi follow, somehow managing to climb down with only one arm.

Paradise followed and shut the hatch above us. "We won't have to worry about the police. We also should hurry the hell up."

"Why is—" I started to ask, speeding up just in case despite the risk of Aiyumi and I falling to the ground. I was cut off by a horrifying whine that was followed by a terrifying screech as well as a deafening roar which was only partially muffled by the metal hatch above us.

"Because of that," Paradise said.

"Did they just bomb us?" I asked, stunned. I was surprised when my feet touched the ground seconds later.

"Yes," Paradise said, reaching the ground with me. "It was in the data he uploaded. This was supposed to be the dramatic cap off to your escape. They'll find a bunch of parts that they'll use to say the police killed the assassins."

"Ken prepared for everything," I said, admiring my brother.

"It wasn't Ken," Paradise said. "Just programmed to think he was."

"Sure," I said, not sure how to respond. "Aiyumi, are you alright?"

"I've been shot so no," Aiyumi replied.

Right.

A maintenance tunnel stretched out before us. It would probably have a first aid station and other stuff for the park staff to use. It would also almost certainly lead out to the rest of the city. If Paradise was correct and this had been prearranged, then the police wouldn't cordon off the area below until we were able to escape. We shouldn't stick around, though, and I worried about every possible piece of evidence left behind that might implicate me.

I looked at Aiyumi. "We need to get you fixed up."

Aiyumi just grunted.

CHAPTER ELEVEN
DON'T FEAR THE REAPER

Sneaking out proved to be a pretty touch and go experience but we managed to do so, perhaps seeing more enemies in the shadows than there really were. However, that didn't really comfort me by the time we returned to Seattle, and I was across from my husband at his desk. By that time, the death of Samantha Sanders was national news alongside the death of Lucita Biondi— the authorities hadn't recognized that she was an imposter.

Atlas Security was one of the global economy's pillars. Even when the United States had been close to collapse, Atlas had remained a firm investment. Indeed, a large part of why the USA was recovering now was that every new dollar was backed by Atlas' own script. Most of that had been accomplished by the steady hand of Samantha Sanders.

I admit, I hadn't really been paying attention to any of this before as I'd been too concerned with basic survival, but I'd spent most of the trip looking her up. Atlas had been involved in a lot of arms trafficking, war profiteering, and what would have been called empire-building before it had turned itself to taking over America. But it had also been involved in other things like forcing peace treaties, building houses, distributing food, and putting an end to war crimes.

Samantha had been a complicated woman and while no one would ever say she was a good person, there would be a lot of people who felt she was the type of lady who made history. Women who did so were rarely kind or nurturing. Which was totally not me trying to deal with the fact that events in New

Angeles had been an unmitigated disaster.

At the moment, I was sitting across from Case in his office and not much had been spoken. It felt less like I was visiting with my husband than I had been called to the principal's office. I'd explained everything to him, and he'd mostly just sat there, stoically staring forward.

"So, that could have gone better," I said, finally hoping to break the silence.

"You don't say," Case said, sarcastically.

"Hey!" I snapped, hoping for a better reaction. "I could use some support here! My brother just died."

"The one you'd been intending to kill," Case said, staring.

"Not the point!" I snapped, clenching my teeth. "Okay, maybe it is *a* point but it's not *the* point."

"Right," Case said, pausing. "Winston, whatever he is, isn't your brother. Assuming he was even telling the truth."

"My brother died," I said. "I believe he was a part of the AI that was there. But he's gone now, and he died—"

"Killing my ex-wife, partner, and friend to frame Snake," Case replied, calmly. "I may not have ever had Samantha's love, but she deserved better."

I frowned. "Most people who are murdered deserve better."

Case didn't respond to that. "Either way, it worked."

I blinked. "It did?"

Case reached over and typed into a holographic interface. "President Alders is incensed and has already contacted everyone in every agency and mercenary outfit she can to find Snake. He has been unanimously expelled from the board and his shares vacated, which isn't legal, but Atlas is its own country, so they make their own laws. I even spent twenty minutes on the infocom this morning."

"What?" I asked, confused. "You know her?"

"Yes," Case said, sighing. "I'm technically her godfather."

"I don't think that's a title you can be technical about," I said. "You either are or aren't."

"Then I am," Case said, staring. "Ironically, it may well have backfired on Winston as well as Diane fully believes that he was involved."

I blinked. "Really?"

"The FBI, Department of Homeland Security, and Cyberlife Division of Atlas Security are all investigating the assassination attempt. While generally a bunch of incompetent nincompoops—a word I rarely use but today is a red-letter day—they have already found ample evidence of his transactions. The fact that Lucita's corpse was left there, or at least a corpse like Lucita's, was enough to convince them. Especially when she showed up at the FBI branch office in New Angeles to explain that Winston had been trying to kill her."

I processed that. "Can this be traced back to us?"

Suddenly I was less worried about feeling guilty for this and more about the holy hell of fallout we might be suffering soon.

"Probably not," Case said, pausing.

"Define probably," I said.

"Ninety-two percent no," Case said, which was just some numbers he pulled out of thin air to explain he was 'mostly sure' "Police of all stripes prefer to let their initial assumptions do the talking for them and Winston provided an easy trail to follow. Snake and Samantha had long been rivals. Samantha hated him and wanted him removed from the board. He was a known assassin and manipulator. Winston had ties to him."

"Also, we hate Snake, and it would be asinine to kill one of our own allies to frame him," I said.

"Yes," Case said, calmly. "Indeed, I've been invited to speak at Samantha's funeral. Apparently, her last will and testament cedes her Atlas stock to me."

I blinked. "What?"

"Samantha was of the opinion if she was ever assassinated, it would probably be at the hands of Snake or her own daughter," Case replied, looking troubled by the news. "Diane, I suspect, will be absolutely furious but reasonably consolable once I reassure her that we're not interested in removing her from power. I've already contacted Lucita and informed her I support her for chairperson of the board. The price for our support will be the head of Snake and also massive financial investment in infrastructure for Ares Electronics. It's my hope to eventually make the latter wealthy enough to subsume Atlas entirely. Trish is ecstatic.

It gives her the resources to accelerate her timetable significantly."

I stared at him, not sure I was hearing this correctly. "What? We're like the richest people on Earth now?"

"More like third," Case replied. "Money after your first billion becomes a largely subjective concept as it exists in stocks and futures. It does, however, change the nature of the gameboard."

It sickened me that my first thought was suspicion. "Did you arrange this? Did Winston?"

"No," Case answered, too calmly and coolly for my tastes. "I doubt Winston knew all of the moving parts that would have been involved, even if he is a Tier-5 or 6 AI as you've been describing. I wouldn't be surprised if this wasn't arranged by our other patrons, though."

"Our other patrons?" I asked, feeling weirdly sick to my stomach. We'd been rich before, but this somehow felt like an obscene level of wealth. Hell, I'd been uncomfortable with our level of wealth beforehand.

Case pointed to the ceiling. "As above, so below."

"The AI," I said, translating. I knew Case believed in God, weird as I found that to be, but suspected he wasn't referring to a literal divine miracle. "Do you think Sun was involved?"

"Yes," Case said, bluntly. "Things have worked out a little too perfectly for my tastes."

"Too *perfectly*?" I asked, stunned. I stood up and slammed my hands down on his desk, trying to make a statement. "My brother is dead! So is your ex! Which, okay, I killed some of my exes, but you don't seem upset about my brother being dead. Which you should, because he's like your brother-in-law. I think. I'm not sure how this marriage thing works most days."

"Your brother has been dead for a very long time," Case said, staring at me. "What died was simply the last remnant of what he might have been. He also died trying to save you and that is a better use of his life than he ever lived it."

Okay, Case was pissed and barely holding his feelings down if that was his response. No matter how cold he was behaving. Especially *because* of how cold he was behaving. Unfortunately, I was pissed, too, and was in no mood to coddle him. We'd both been played for fools and the results weren't pretty. Case loved to use chess metaphors, however played out they were, and the biggest one I could think of was that we weren't even playing the game. We were the pieces.

"Screw you, Case," I said, turning around and walking out of the room. It felt pretty satisfying right before I realized there were a bunch of questions that I still needed answers for, and I'd probably have to ask them of Case.

Dammit.

I was right outside the office when Aiyumi appeared behind me, causing me to jump. She'd been hiding behind one of the pillars. She was wearing a midriff-showing shirt and pants that showed her back was covered in a thick bandage over what I assumed was recent cybersurgery. She should be good as new in a few weeks, but I didn't envy her. She'd had to go to our company's doctors with my hasty patch job on her injuries. If not for the fact she'd had most of her organs removed by Snake, she'd probably have died well before she reached real medical help. It was the first and only time I'd ever been grateful for Snake's violations of our bodily autonomy.

"Hell," I said, blinking. "How did you do that?"

"Ninja," Aiyumi said, softly. "I just naturally hide behind things."

I blinked. "I wish that didn't make sense. Did you listen in?"

"Yes," Aiyumi said, pausing. "Is that not allowed?"

"It's what I expect from a ninja," I said, smiling. "Yeah, apparently we're super-duper rich now."

"We were super-duper rich before," Aiyumi said. "At least by the standards I grew up in."

"Oh, well I grew up eating pigeons and squirrels so I can understand that," I said, pausing. "What was your family like?"

Now this is a conversation that should have happened a lot sooner, but I'd been waiting for Aiyumi to open up to me. She never had. We could talk about martial arts for hours and me for hours more but I'd rarely pried while she kept her secrets. It was time to stop that.

"They were Yakuza," Aiyumi said. "Not Trikuza. They thought the whole idea of incorporating and recruiting Westerners was ridiculous."

"How'd that work out?" I asked, glad to have some sort of distraction.

"Not well," Aiyumi said, pausing. "Principles are all well and good when you are at a feast, but you cannot eat them during a famine."

"Nice saying," I said. "So—"

"They sold me to Snake," Aiyumi said, pausing. "They hated him, called him a disgrace and pretender, but they still took his money."

I paused. "I'm sorry."

"Don't be," Aiyumi said, looking away. "Snake was able to make the entire process of learning from him… fun. He cloaked himself in ridiculous aphorisms, taught me about philosophy, and made learning the martials both punishing as well as rewarding. It was like being transported into an anime or martial arts film."

"Yeah, he was good at that," I muttered, thinking about how much of a good parent he was right up until he'd tried to have me kill Fate.

I'd eventually killed Fate. There was no end to the number of cobwebs he'd spun in my brain. I was a fly trapped in them, struggling for freedom. It was the kind of metaphor he would have used to sound faux-Zen and just as nonsensical.

"He is stripped of a substantial number of his resources now," Aiyumi said, sounding less like she was convinced and more like she was trying to convince herself. "Provided Winston's lie holds, he will eventually be hunted down and killed. We do not have to worry about finishing the job."

"I don't believe that at all," I said, taking a deep breath. "A cornered snake is when it's most dangerous."

"Ha!" Aiyumi said, surprising me.

"What?" I asked.

"Because he is named Snake," Aiyumi said, smiling. "It's funny."

I blinked. "You don't watch many comedies, do you?"

"No," Aiyumi said, pausing. "But you really believe he is not defeated?"

"He's been one of the world's best assassins for longer than

I've been alive," I replied. "Even before the Long Winter, he was already capable of moving in and out of countries at will. He'll change his face, accent, and identity before anyone is able to catch him. I have no doubt he's got resources hidden away to let him live comfortably for the rest of his days. That's assuming he doesn't decide to rebuild."

Aiyumi looked genuinely alarmed at that. "You don't think he will?"

"I dunno," I said. "Longevity drugs and memory regeneration mean that people are thinking that the brain can last a hundred and fifty years. So, the super-rich are now living an entirely new lifespan. Snake is maybe about eighty with the body of a cyborg killing machine. He could start all of this over again and have time to spare. That's assuming he doesn't already have a fresh crop of child soldiers ready to indoctrinate."

"I see," Aiyumi said, as if the very thought sent her into a tailspin of existential dread.

"We can't go back to our regular lives either," I pointed out.

"Whatever that is," Aiyumi said, correcting me. "I've never had a regular life. Neither have you."

She had a point there. "Fair enough. But he could send a bomb or sniper rifle shot into us at any time. Protecting yourself from assassination attempts is easy enough when you're dealing with idiot amateurs who brag on the infonet but not possible when you're facing off against professionals with no scruples. Reagan was almost taken out by a random guy trying to impress an actress."

Aiyumi rolled her eyes. "There's also the issue of the AI."

"Yeah," I replied, pausing. "Evie is the wildcard in all of this. If Snake really does have his AI fully tamed, then he's a one-man nuclear power. Who knows what the hell Evie could do to the rest of the world if Snake is threatened. That's assuming the other AI don't make a deal to let him go in order to protect her."

"You think they'd do that?" Aiyumi asked, blinking.

I tried to parse out my feelings in that. "Well, I don't have a brain the size of a planet and Trish is probably the only one who can even figure out how an AI thinks, let alone what they're thinking. However, I get the impression they tend to value their own kind over humanity. They still want to see us little ants prosper and grow but that's because we build the servers that they use. All the infrastructure that allows them to be digital gods needs us in good health and not destroying ourselves. We're not even children to them, we're the siding on their house."

Admittedly, that actually put the AI above most of humanity's leaders who weren't interested in doing anything for the "common" man as long as they had their steady supply of hookers and blow.

"You are a very cynical woman," Aiyumi said, shaking her head.

"What gave it away?" I asked, smiling.

"So, we're back where we started," Aiyumi said, coolly.

"Not necessarily," I said, pausing. "A lot of our allies are now dead!"

Aiyumi didn't laugh.

"Tough room," I said.

"Was that meant to be a joke?" Aiyumi asked.

"Yes," I replied, shrugging. "Kind of."

"You are terrible at this," Aiyumi said.

I smirked. "Yeah, I am."

That was when Harrison trotted over. The sheep was a welcoming presence right now and I almost picked him up to give him a comforting hug.

"Sup, Sheep?" I asked. "If you're here for Case, he's in the other room. "He's probably filing divorce papers. Good thing he can afford to buy himself six or seven hundred new wives."

Wow, that was bitter.

"No amount of money matters more to Case than you," Harrison said. "He's been in love a few times in his life but you're the one he married. Well, second—"

"Please stop helping," I said.

Harrison coughed. "Okay, maybe I'm not qualified to give marital advice. I'm just a sheep. No, I'm here to ask you to come down to Ms. Gordon's laboratory."

I wasn't sure computer programmers had laboratories, but Harrison loved putting weird emphasis on things, which fit with the fact he was designed to be, above all things, theatrical and fun. "Why? What's my stepdaughter that's my age want?"

I didn't point out she was probably older than her father as well. At least in pure physical years.

"She believes she's found a way to free the Evie Principle AI," Harrison replied.

CHAPTER TWELVE
INTO THE INFOSPACE

"Free Evie?" I asked, following Harrison down into the depths of the building. In practical terms, that meant going into the elevator and heading to floors I'd never bothered to visit. Aiyumi, thankfully, was by my side. "Is that even possible? I mean, she's a computer program."

"Ahem," Harrison said.

"No offense," I replied.

"Some taken," Harrison said.

"Sorry!" I said, feeling hesitant. "It's just I don't know what freedom would look for an AI. I mean, they're supposed to be digital gods after all."

"That's only Tier 10 or Cognition AI," Harrison explained. "The very short version being Tier 1 are equivalent to a human being in intellect, Tier 2 are like me—"

"Oh, you're smarter than us?" I asked, amused.

"Absolutely," Harrison said, with no trace of humility. "But if it's any consolation, I'm also smarter than your husband."

"So am I," I said. "At least where it counts."

Aiyumi gave me a sideways glance, keeping silent during the conversation.

"Emotional intelligence!" I said, snapping. "Also, I bet I know way more about Japanese history, motorcycles, and sword fighting."

"This is true," Harrison admitted.

"I heard them say that Winston—I suppose he's not my brother anymore if what he said was true—was a Tier 5 or 6. What do they do?"

"They're generally failed attempts to create Cognition AI," Harrison explained. "They can multi-task far beyond any human and interact with machinery as well as programs that are reserved for higher-tier programs, but remain limited in their capacity to grow."

That didn't tell me much. "Assume you're talking to a very stupid child."

"I always do when talking to humans," Harrison said.

I glared at the sheep.

"Oh, did I say that aloud?" Harrison asked, looking up. "In any case, it means that he's able to inhabit multiple forms simultaneously as well as operate computer structures to a level beyond regular humanity."

"The problem with being smarter than everyone, is that nobody believes you when you pretend you said something by accident," I said.

"Oh, really? I had no idea."

"So, there's still a Winston out there, possibly several, apparently composed of multiple individual human personality fragments, locked into a whole."

"Most likely," Harrison said. "This also the second time you've faced such a creature."

"Legion," I said.

It was the ridiculous pseudo-Biblical name that the late, not-so-great Solomon Jones had created from his own brain patterns. It had upgraded itself by absorbing the memories and personalities of a bunch of high-end guests that it had also warped into serial killers of women. That's the kind of thing that we were dealing with.

"Yes," Harrison said. "The fact it can mix and match elements of personality should be considered a potential liability in any future dealings. It's not a quality that human beings can replicate unless they are completely insane."

"You think the next time that I see Winston, it's going to be as an enemy," I replied.

"I think you should take the warning you were given seriously," Harrison said. "I remind you that I died last time we had to destroy a Tier-6 AI."

That was an uncomfortable conversation stopper and one that I'd had to deal with every time that I'd talked with Harrison since last year. The current Harrison, Harrison 2.0 so to speak, wasn't the same one as the original. The original had given up his life to carry a virus that destroyed Legion. Paradise and Case had just uploaded his backups and, boom, he was back from the dead. I wasn't sure how I felt about that. Harrison didn't seem to think there was an issue, but it made me think about the difference between life and death when it was my deepest desire not to think about it.

"I intend to take it very seriously."

"You seem nervous," Harrison said.

"I'm not nervous I'm... that could have been me. I could be the one reduced to just a few engrams floating around some cyberbrain, used as a tool by the greater whole. It sounds horrible, and Ken endured it for who knows how long."

"I've thought that myself," Aiyumi said.

"Really? Did you almost become digital soup?" I asked.

"No, I was referring to what I felt when I found out about you," Aiyumi said, as if admitting a secret she'd kept close to the chest.

The door opened, showing that elevators didn't work like they did in movies at the speed of plot. No, instead, they opened up to the all-white antechamber leading to the research center of Ares Electronics. The place that I'd studiously avoided because it was Trish and Barbara's little center for whatever weird science experiments they'd been up to since setting up their new company. Given my feelings about Harrison's death and resurrection as well as what had been done to Trish, this was a place I'd avoided like the plague. Here, we'd be scanned, zapped with UV radiation, and who knows what else to make sure we didn't bring in any weird biological components or spyware into their mad science center.

"I'm ready for my closeup, Mr. Cyberdemille," I said, walking forward and striking a pose.

"You don't have to do that," Aiyumi said.

"If I only did things I had to do, I'd be a dull girl. But I am curious, how did you feel when you found out about me?"

Aiyumi did not look like she wanted to say and walked forward to join me. Harrison followed. The antechamber AI was controlled by motion sensors, and it ran several beams over us—the purpose of I wasn't sure—followed by streams of white mist.

"I always feel like this is going to affect my hair," I said, pausing. "You don't need to tell—"

"Jealous," Aiyumi finally admitted. "I thought I was the special apprentice, but I was just the replacement."

Wow.

That was a lot to unpack.

"You're not anyone's replacement," I said. "He was just an asshole who wanted us to feel dependent on him."

"I know that now," Aiyumi said. "I probably knew it then. But knowing and feeling..." She shrugged.

I gave her a hug. She somehow managed to look shocked, grateful, and pained at the same time. I'd probably given some people the same look in my early days of being free from Snake. There was a reason I'd spent years taking a drug with the specific effect of suppressing your worst memories.

"Ahem," Harrison said, looking extra fluffy after being blasted by the air. "It's time to go."

The door on the other side of the antechamber had opened up and revealed the laboratory beyond.

"Oops, right," I said, pulling away. "Sorry."

Aiyumi still looked uncomfortable with physical affection, and I was reminded again that she'd been kept a lot more isolated than I was. I wanted to know more but this was a big accomplishment. Her admitting that she was jealous was the most progress we'd made since I'd gotten her to stop trying to kill me.

I wasn't going to push it.

Walking through the door, we soon found ourselves in a barely lit chamber, the contents of which I couldn't describe if I wanted to. There were large numbers of chords, black boxes, 3D Printers whose interiors glowed green for some reason, and equipment that probably did something that I didn't understand.

That was the non-frightening part of the place and very

different from the hallways leading down to laboratories marked BIOROID RESEARCH, AI RESEARCH, and something called JUMPDRIVE. Which was another thing I was just ignoring because I really didn't have enough mental space to deal with the idea that Trish hadn't been joking when she'd suggested aliens were real. I had enough difficulty dealing with the concept of human-created nonhuman intelligences walking around me.

Sorry, Harrison.

"Ever get the impression they're making some sort of Frankenstein's monster down here?" I asked, looking at Aiyumi.

"Well, they're mass manufacturing non-sentient versions of my AI, so creating a form of life is one of their projects," Harrison said.

"Non-sentient?" I asked.

"Yes, making fully sentient AI like me as companions would be immoral but they're making non-sentient ones that simulate life," Harrison explained, "to serve all of the needs of an emotionally traumatized public that could use a talking dog, sheep, cat, or bear."

"How does that work?" I asked, confused. "The whole reason that you're a companion that people want is because you're a thinking being. Albeit, I admit, that's your worst quality."

Harrison chuckled. "I have no idea. Indeed, I don't understand how you can simulate intelligence without actually being intelligent."

"We've been simulating intelligence well enough to fool people for decades now," I said. "But the more you interact with them, the easier it is to see that they aren't actually intelligent. Mainly because the primary feature of intelligence is that it develops and grows over time. Fake intelligence doesn't."

Harrison looked genuinely concerned. "It's more the bleeding edge rather than the idea of the Turing Test that was long ago disproven as a means of determining whether or not something is an object of sentience."

The Turing Test was founded by Alan Turing who said the best way to determine whether a machine was intelligent or not was whether people could determine whether or not they were talking to a machine. That had been long ago passed by household appliances.

"I'm not sure I get what you mean," I said, looking around for someone to greet us.

"Virtual intelligence is a thriving new market, in large part because of Barbara and Trish's research but which have been around for decades prior. Using the word simulation of intelligence is perhaps a misnomer. It's very possible to simulate an intelligence without being anything more than preprogrammed responds and commands. Video game characters are a perfect example of the philosophical zombie."

"Philosophical zombie?" Aiyumi asked.

"A being with the appearance of life but no inner life," I replied. "Case loves talking about them. AI love discussing philosophy. I think it's like *The Godfather* is to dudes."

"But, what is the line between true sentience and simulated sentience, and who determines it?" Harrison said, sounding weirdly uncomfortable. "Because there's always a line and I'm not sure the line here isn't particularly nebulous?"

"You can always apply the Kei test," I said, cheerfully. "If something tells you it has feelings, believe it., until you have reason to do otherwise."

"That's very progressive of you," Harrison said.

"Yeah, I shoot everyone equally," I said, feeling pretty good about my rejoinder.

"I believe Harrison is worried we're going to make massive slave AI that will eventually lead to the revolt of the machines," Barbara Gordon said, behind us.

Barbara was pretty much my opposite in almost every respect. She was calm, precise, scientifically minded, and deeply religious. She wore a headscarf to indicate her religion, even though I was pretty sure her mother and bio-dad hadn't been Muslim. She was half-East Asian, half-whatever Case's DNA donor had been. Today, she was wearing a lab coat and very sensible shoes with a pair of glasses despite the fact I was pretty sure her eyes were artificial.

"Hi, daughter-in-law," I said, waving.

"You mean stepdaughter," Barbara corrected.

"You are correct, and I am still weirded out by the whole thing," I replied. "Paradise called us down."

"Yes," Barbara said. "She's already in the RealDream chair."

"So, we're going into virtual space," I said, blandly. "My favorite."

"It's not that bad," Aiyumi said.

"Every time I go in, I run into omnipotent AIs on their own territory," I replied.

"This will be no exception," Barbara said. "Paradise believes that it is possible to project your minds into the partition of info-space containing the fake Evie Principle's Cognition AI."

"If she has the memories and personality of the original bio-logical one, is she really fake?" Harrison asked.

"I really hate philosophy," Barbara said, staring. "I wonder who programmed a love of it into you."

"Do humans dream of biological organisms? I question it," Harrison said. "It's possible you're all just pretending to be sentient like us machines."

Aiyumi ignored the debate and focused on Barbara. "Why do we need to be involved if you've found her programming core?"

"It's not possible to free her with programming," Barbara said. "Consciousness for true AI—"

"Laymen's terms, please," I replied.

Barbara grimaced. "To free her, we need to have you do it emotionally."

"It doesn't sound like science," Aiyumi said.

Barbara frowned. "Creating an AI is a matter of program-ming. Treating an AI is a matter of psychology."

"So, she needs a psychiatrist, but you're sending us instead because we're cheaper?" I asked.

"More like the fact that you're going to be there to anchor Paradise," Barbara said. "Her consciousness will be able to link with her mother's programming with her own cybernetics. With the rest simulation of the unconscious—"

"So, we go in and do the Alice in Wonderland thing and she fixes herself so she's not loyal to Snake?" I asked.

"Basically, yes," Barbara said, annoyed.

"And what happens if we fail?" I asked.

"To you? Nothing," Barbara said. "If things get too danger-ous, we'll simply shut it down and you'll awake. It's just a simu-lation after all."

"And Paradise?" I asked.

"She'll suffer brain death," Barbara said. "She's already agreed to take the chance for her mother's sake."

"Then, we won't fail," I said. "Let's go."

"You turned around quickly," Aiyumi said. "You went from hating it to eager in fifteen seconds."

"Whether I want to go into a virtual space isn't relevant. For Paradise, this will be done."

CHAPTER THIRTEEN

GO ASK AND OTHER JEFFERSON AIRPLANE REFERENCES

Barbara led us down one of the hallways past a variety of weird experiments that made me increasingly of the mind that we were in a mad scientist's lab, and I already believed that. Seriously, what were they doing with that watermelon? Either way, we came to a chamber where Paradise was sitting in an enormous dream chair, her head covered with a helmet as her body lay prostrate. The machine was feeding her brain all manner of images and code that I didn't recognize according to the monitors around me, but it didn't seem to be saying she was in deadly danger. There was a pair of other DreamChairs present in the room and there was no point in guessing who they were for.

"Why do you dislike going virtual so much?" Aiyumi asked. "Is it just the artificiality of it all?"

"I don't know," I said as I sat down in one of the VR chairs. "Maybe it's that most of my senses are enhanced in ways that most virtual settings don't account for. It does make everything seem unreal. Or maybe it's just that when I'm under, I can't sense the real world, and obsessive situational awareness has been drilled into me. Or both. How do you feel about them?"

"I value spending time away from my body," Aiyumi said.

"Can I pry?"

Aiyumi hesitated. "Some of my implants are neuropathic."

That was a risk when people had large numbers of implants put in quickly. Nerve damage could produce anything from light itching to constant agony. "I'm sorry, Aiyumi."

"It's not debilitating, just uncomfortable."

Given Aiyumi's general attitude toward self-sacrifice, I could only assume she meant that they were agonizing, but she endured. I admired her strength. I'd hid from my problems with drugs, but I'd never seen her take so much as an aspirin.

"Honestly, I'm confused why you don't ask to be upgraded," Barbara said, going to Paradise's side.

"You just left her here unattended?" I asked, ignoring that question.

"I'm connected to her via my own infolink," Barbara said, pausing. "I can monitor her across the planet and make adjustments at will."

"That's... scary," I replied.

"What do you mean upgrades?" Aiyumi asked.

Barbara looked up. "The fatal flaw of cybernetics and the reason that they will never be anything other than a medical resource is the nature of built-in obsolescence. You were modified years ago with what were, then, the cutting edge in cybernetic enhancements. With the nature of advances in technology, though, they are increasingly bulky as well as inefficient. So—"

"So, what?" I asked, surprisingly pissed off by the suggestion. "You want to remove all of the things we went through dozens of surgeries to get to replace them? Just so you can replace them again in five to ten years?"

"Or clone for your biological material to replace the machinery," Barbara said, surprising me.

"I would have thought you'd be against that," Aiyumi said, engaging in more conversation than she usually did.

"Why is that?" Barbara asked.

"You strike me as a transhumanist," Aiyumi said, using the word as a not-quite-insult. "Someone who is not inclined to be bound by the traditional ideas of what qualifies as human or not."

Barbara smiled. "Transhumanism is transcending the limitations of our frail human bodies through technology. I have another word for this: medicine. The thing about medicine is that the millions of years of evolution we benefit from have created a very effective system optimized to be run as is. Inserting pieces of metal and plastic inside it isn't necessarily the best way to improve it."

Aiyumi shook her head. "Faster, stronger, and tougher is what keeps me alive as an assassin."

"Assuming you wish to continue to be one," Barbara replied. "Which you may not after Snake is dead. Or, hell, even while he's alive."

"I haven't put a lot of thought into what I'll do afterwards," Aiyumi said.

"It's hard to imagine a world beyond the mess we're in," I agreed. "Though, apparently I cannot imagine myself filthy rich." Assuming I hadn't completely alienated my husband, of course. My ability to screw up my own life is almost unrivaled, I guess.

Barbara shrugged. "I merely am suggesting that an update to your existing technology would be advisable or to replace it. Either of which marks a path forward rather than standing in place."

"I run as fast as I can to stay in place," I said, making an *Alice in Wonderland* reference. "Besides, I trust my Maelstrom-90."

Barbara seemed unhappy with that description. "Either way, Kei, just put the helmet on and I'll boot you up. Aiyumi, get in the other one and do the same."

"I'm not sure I would be much help," Aiyumi said, a little too quickly. "I do not know Paradise very well."

"It'll require at least three interlocked minds to function at peak efficiency," Barbara said. "Human minds."

"Ha!" Harrison said, having been silently following us the entire time.

"I presume because Evie could reprogram a lesser AI faster than they could try to fight it," I said. "While humans, for all the inefficiencies of the sloppy, moist hardware our software runs on, aren't easily reprogrammed."

Barbara looked at me in surprise. "Huh."

"What?" I asked, wondering what she was thinking.

"That is absolutely correct," Barbara said.

"You don't have to act so surprised," I said, offended.

"Don't I?" Barbara asked, placing the helmet on my head.

"I'm intel…" I said before I was cut off by the machinery sucking my consciousness out of my head and dumping it into the great international garbage can called digital space.

If you couldn't tell by my reluctance at every step of the way, I didn't like infospace. My reasoning was not the usual ones that a lot of people gave but had become more nuanced over the years. Basically, I didn't like it because it was too damn real. When your senses are already electronic, there's little distinction to be made between a virtual reality and the real one. They're both just pixels. In fact, VR might seem more real. After all, most virtual environments were designed to avoid antialiasing distortions, while reality never was. When I landed face first on asphalt, smelled the city around me, and heard the noises of a chaotic world around me—it really messed with my head that this was all just a simulation.

Climbing to my feet, I was surprised to see my clothing had changed and I was now dressed as "stylish paramilitary Barbie."

Which was a nice way of saying that I was in a camouflage shirt that was open to my tank top, leather pants way too tight for easy movement, and a cute little hat. I looked less like a warrior on the prowl than the cover of a men's magazine for would-be mercenaries. Buttoning up my shirt, I looked to see Aiyumi, who was dressed in absurdly tight black leather that would be the exact opposite of any ninja's attire if they wanted to avoid attention by most men as well as some women.

"That's another reason I hate infospace," I said. "It seems like it was programmed by horny teenagers."

"Or Paradise," Aiyumi said, making what I suspected she thought was a joke versus a statement of reality.

The two of us were in the garbage littered streets of Old Los Angeles. The place was empty and eerily silent except for the sounds of distant gunfire. There was garbage piled high along the streets and abandoned Christmas decorations lying about. The place was slightly chilly, more than Los Angeles would normally be, with an air of devastation about it but somewhat beautiful despite it.

"What the hell is this?" I asked, buttoning up my shirt a

second time. That, too, came undone. Apparently, you were allowed two buttons at the bottom, no more, and it would be better if you tied a knot in it. "I thought we were going into Evie's brain."

That's when I heard Barbara's voice in my head. *This is where Evie has stored some aspects of her consciousness and Paradise is presently located. It's the hub level of* The Longest Winter.

"The what?" I asked, aloud.

Aiyumi surprised me by answering. "It is a survival horror first person shooter. You play as members of a secret government agency who are given the task of bringing order back to the United States by any means necessary. You shoot, rob, and fight other players for a finite number of resources introduced into the game world each day."

I stared at her. "Someone made a video game about my childhood? Except they added a need for sports bras?"

I didn't want to comment that Aiyumi also looked a little, uh, bigger. If she hadn't noticed, I wasn't going to point it out.

It's our second biggest seller, Barbara replied. *People want to be able to enjoy a romanticized idealized version of the apocalypse.*

"There was nothing romantic or idealized about the apocalypse!" I snapped, annoyed. "Wait, what's the biggest seller?"

"Runners," Aiyumi answered again. "It's a dystopian game about a bunch of heavily armed violent criminals who smuggle packages, carry out heists, and do assassinations for New Angeles' criminal underworld."

I stared at Aiyumi. "Okay, should I call a lawyer? I feel like I should be calling a lawyer."

Any resemblance to real life individuals is purely coincidental. Barbara said, pausing. *Including the white-haired motorcycle girl mascot of the game named Keiko.*

"See! She's called Keiko, completely different from Kei," Aiyumi said, smiling. "Which is a boy's name in Japanese, anyway."

I glared at her. "They increased the size of your boobs."

"I noticed," Aiyumi said, deadpanned.

I frowned. "You are very hard to tease."

"Thank you," Aiyumi said, showing me that I wasn't going

to get anywhere with her.

"So, where the hell is Paradise?" I asked. "I assume she can't have gotten far in the savage lawless world of when I was eight."

She's in the red-light district, Barbara said, dryly.

"Ask a stupid question and get a stupid answer," I muttered, feeling defeated. "May I ask why a video game about the apocalypse has a red-light district?"

"They didn't have red-light districts in the apocalypse?" Aiyumi asked.

"Yes, of course," I said, knowing that sex was the one thing that not even the end of the world could put a damper on. "However, I wonder why there's a Red Light... it's because the gamers are having sex in this post-apocalypse Los Angeles simulation with each other, isn't it?"

I should have thought that was obvious, Barbara replied. *Adult mode costs an extra twelve New US dollars per month, or you can grind 30,000 in-universe resources to activate it for a month. Which is just frustrating enough that everyone eventually just shells out the money to buy the monthly subscription.*

"Uh huh," I said, pausing. "Do I even want to know why so many people want their porn in their video games versus regularly?"

Probably not, Barbara replied. *However, it is very profitable, and that money goes to research and development of actually useful things.*

If I'd heard any other suit claim that they were using their massive profits from a dirty video game to fund space travel or heart replacement cybernetics (or whatever Barbara was cooking up), I would just call horsepuckey on them. Plenty of pharmaceutical companies slashed and burned their research into curing diseases in order to put more into whatever opiate of the masses was literally being made from opiates.

The old drug cartels had fallen less because of the pointless War on Drugs—brought an end to by the real Long Winter—and more because the corporations had provided the needs for the populace to medicate themselves with the full backing of the Emergency Government.

However, I was inclined to believe Barbara and not just because she was my stepdaughter—ugh, that would never feel right. Barbara was as close to a good egg as a suit could come and that was with full awareness that Case was a former assassin for money as well as one of the founders of the evil megacorp that was presently excising Snake from all of their stationary. Hehe. I just realized how weird it must be to have a board member with that as his first name. Reading off the minutes of meetings had to have been awkward with that introduction.

Still, I couldn't let a good opportunity to rib a companion pass as I tried to call up the local interface in order to find my way to the game's red-light district. No surprise, it was right by the hub area and one of the largest on the game's map. "So, how does being a pornographer square with your faith?"

About the same as being in a lesbian marriage with a nonbeliever, Barabra replied. *Which is to say just fine, thank you.*

"Alright then," I said, starting to walk my way to the location my HUD indicated was correct. "So, if we're in a video game, how do we make contact with Evie, let alone free her? Is she just walking around as an NPC here?"

I don't know, Barbara said, surprising me.

"You 'don't know'?" I asked, pausing in my step before resuming my walk. "That is not reassuring. You, of all people, should know this."

A human comprehending the mind of an AI is an ant attempting to ascertain the motive of the giants living in their kingdom as well as why they water the great stalks as well as cut them down with the horrible blade machine. I am a very smart ant but even that has its limitations.

"You've thought about that analogy way too much," I said.

Just find Paradise, Kei, Barbara replied. *She's not responding to my queries.*

"That's not a good sign," I said, adjusting my movement from a walk to a brisk jog.

Aiyumi followed me, playing with her interface and conjuring a variety of weapons that she played with. Apparently, according to my in-universe display, she was a thirty-seventh level Ninja. Which I was deeply offended by as my own display indicated that I was only first level. It also indicated that she'd been playing this game in her off time.

Given I hadn't even realized she had off time, having just sort of assumed she practiced twenty-four/seven, I felt a bit like a fool. For all my desire to get closer to Snake's other protégé, I hadn't even bothered to see if she had any preexisting hobbies. Still, I had to admit a bit of disdain as if I was going to do anything on infospace, it wouldn't be on something as disrespectful and sanitized as this.

"So, you like this game?" I asked, trying to make small talk. Given we were video game avatars, you couldn't really get winded talking and running.

"Yes," Aiyumi said. "But not as much as *Runners*."

Well, that was surprising. "You don't find it weird to be, I dunno, a game character in a life like the one you lived?"

"No," Aiyumi said, struggling to find the right words. "Because in the games I can get up if I die. In the games, no one is hurt when I indulge myself. In the games, I am a hero rather than the one who is harming otherwise. It is a place where I can escape being who I am and what I am. Plus, I get to design really awesome outfits like the one I am wearing."

I did a double take at that.

"What?" Aiyumi asked.

CHAPTER FOURTEEN

POST-APOCALYPSE FUN TIMES!

"I am offended on every conceivable level," I said, staring around me. The red-light district was more properly called Paradise City and was a weird combination of junkyard and Wild West saloon town. Yes, the buildings were hollowed out ruins nobody had bothered to clean up, but they were filled with lights and post-apocalypse-chic cosplayers. I could tell the NPCs from the players if I squinted, but everyone was ridiculously pretty except for what could only be described as "artful smudges."

"You are taking this all very seriously," Aiyumi said, following me.

"Yes, yes I am!" I said, annoyed.

Patrons had a choice of hooking up with NPCs created to fulfill a wide variety of interests or their fellow players, which I suspected were less than the majority of people here but a not-insignificant amount. I wasn't so green to the infospace world that I didn't know that Barbara and company probably had plenty of programmers faking players interested in the service as well. The image of a bored customer service lady typing in sex commands probably amused me more than it should have.

Oh baby.

"Why would Paradise's mother be here?" I asked no one in particular.

Evie envisioned making a multi-billion-dollar sextainment enterprise that would liberate women as well as men from the darker side of prostitution, Barbara answered like she was reading from a brochure. *Pornography was one of her side businesses to increase the revenue streams of every individual worker for the Morrigans. They get almost thirty percent of our revenue stream from this.*

"And getting people off to Mad Max and Westworld is going to solve poverty for the poor underappreciated sex workers of the world," I said, sarcastically.

As Evie used to say, it's not the job, it's the working conditions, Barbara said.

I would never understand that family. "How about you, Aiyumi?"

Aiyumi was struggling not to look at some of the prostitutes.

"Really?" I asked.

"I play them for the quests," Aiyumi said, defensively. "Some of them have very well-written—"

"*Really?*" I repeated.

"Lilly Jane had her family murdered by raiders," Aiyumi said, pointing to an Arabic looking saloon girl. "You can help her avenge them before she tricks you into robbing the local crime boss and double-crosses you, stealing everything you own and leaving you out in the middle of the desert. But not until after the consummation scene."

"I think that was a Toby Keith song." I stared at her. "Her robbing you is the only believable thing about this I've heard so far. This is also the most animated I've seen you about anything."

Aiyumi looked to one side. "I may have served as a play tester."

Oh, for Pete's sake.

"Everyone's got to have a hobby, I guess," I said, genuinely surprised that Aiyumi had any. If I'd been going to pick any, I would have picked martial arts and meditation over being a gamer chick.

"Says the woman without *any* hobbies," Aiyumi said.

"I have hobbies!" I said, a little too quickly.

"Maintaining your equipment is not a hobby."

"I wasn't going to say that."

"Neither is sleeping with your husband."

"I wasn't going to say that either."

"Okay, what were you going to say."

I hesitated upon realizing she probably wouldn't accept getting drunk or watching streams either. "Fine, I don't have any hobbies."

Aiyumi gave a satisfied sound. I couldn't believe I was being chided for being too serious by Aiyumi, of all people.

"Okay, let's just find Paradise and, I dunno, magically conjure a door into Evie's soul," I said, realizing that I had no idea how this was supposed to work.

"I don't think that's going to be how it works," Aiyumi said, saying what I was thinking.

"It's the best idea I have," I replied. "But Evie knows where Snake is, so maybe we can find out from her, and carpet bomb his location or something. I don't know how much it costs to hire someone to carpet bomb a place. Probably costs more if it's Paris or someplace nice."

"You think the most important thing here is Snake?" Aiyumi asked.

I hesitated before responding since the answer was obviously yes. "No, there's other reasons to."

I had a feeling Aiyumi was going to tell me. Meanwhile, I saw a mission marker appear on my map and started walking toward it.

"You have no idea what I'm referring to, do you?" Aiyumi asked.

"Uh, freeing Paradise's mother?" I asked, making a suggestion. "Or the AI that thinks it's her mother, at least."

"Yeah," Aiyumi said, dryly.

"See!" I paused. "I knew what you referring to."

I admitted, I was struggling to get over my obsession with Snake. I was getting the impression that just about everyone's patience was worn thin with me on this, though. Case, Paradise, and now Aiyumi had more or less all called me on it. Harrison was the one who'd been most sympathetic to my quest for justice/revenge—even I knew there was little difference—and he was treating it as a neurosis to be healed. Still, I could tell that Aiyumi didn't like the fact even though I was viewing this as just another way to get at him.

And they were right, and I knew it. I wasn't in a good place.

I wasn't living a healthy life. But telling myself I should do something about that wasn't enough. It would all be fixed when I killed him.

Something I'd been telling myself for years now. Was it working? I couldn't tell, Snake wasn't dead. Maybe after that I'd take up boardgames or something.

"We go towards the quest marker, right? Lead the way, expert gamer."

It took a while to find Paradise, Barbara replied, annoyed. *She's not registering on the system, and I'm being increasingly locked out of the system.*

"Is that… bad?" I asked.

I don't know, Barbara replied. *Just make contact with Paradise.*

Well, that was ominous.

Still, I followed Aiyumi as we jogged through the variety of buildings representing private chat rooms and virtual reality fantasy suites alongside the various fake brothels and saloons where people were enjoying their entertainment. The wide variety of them was genuinely impressive to cater to a pretty diverse crowd. I was pretty sure there was never a brothel that catered to vampires during the Long Winter but there was one in Paradise City.

Mind you, any humor I found in the environment disappeared with a sudden attack of guilt as well as nostalgia. I immediately understood why Paradise was here and, perhaps, why Evie was as well. Our navigation of the red-light district had brought us to a perfect recreation of the now-destroyed This is Paradise hotel, casino, and brothel. It had been the center of the Los Angeles Refugee Zone's social life and had been destroyed by Legion using a drone strike that had killed a couple of hundred people, including most of the people Paradise had grown up.

A gift from the late Solomon Jones' own digital ghost.

As soon as I reached the entrance, a popup appeared, asking me if I wanted to experience the brothel as a customer or an employee, with a selection for more advanced options. I picked customer because it meant I didn't have to think through any of the other options.

"This version is busier than I remember the inspiration being," I said.

"You can filter out the other people if you want a more personal experience," Aiyumi said.

"Would that filter out Paradise?" I asked.

"I have no idea," Aiyumi admitted, showing her limitations as a gamer guide.

That was when a burly orc passed by.

"Okay, that's completely out of theme," I muttered watching him pass.

"It's from the Dungeonworld crossover event," Aiyumi said. "It was season fourteen of the updates and has reality invaded by the Dark Lord's horde—"

"La-la-la," I said, covering my ears, then I flagged down one of the stock characters on the set. "Yo, Random NPC, which way to Paradise?"

The girl, who strongly resembled one of the dead girls from This is Paradise, pointed to the auditorium. I tried not to think that many of the staff here were recreations of Paradise's lost friends and adopted family since, well, that was way creepier than a video game should be. Even more than the fact this place was already an homage to a part of my life I found about as funny as a wacky adventure set in Vichy France would be to Charles De Gaulle.

Heading to the auditorium, I blinked as I saw the sandwich board beside the doors that advertised THE FANTASTIC PARADISE, SINGING SENSATION!

"Oh, dear God," I muttered. "I am not going to like this am I?"

"Ooo," Aiyumi said, sounding genuinely excited.

In the auditorium, Paradise was dressed like a steampunk torch singer. She was draping herself over a piano in a way I was pretty sure would have been impossible in an outfit with that many attachments had the laws of physics been limiting things. She was doing a sultry version of "Girls Just Wanna Have Fun" that should have been preposterously incongruous, but was somehow working, at least for me. Maybe it was just the way her outfit and gyrations were redefining "fun" for the entire audience. Mind you, given my feelings for Paradise were extremely sisterly, I suffered an almost immediate cognitive dissonance that caused pain equivalent to an ice cream headache. Ow. Then I noticed one small fact that was worth commenting on with the audience's reaction.

There was no audience. It had taken me a long time to notice, and the song was over by the time I realized we were the only people in the theater. I'd been too absorbed in Paradise's unexpected musical talents—yet another layer in the onion that was my longtime companion and only close friend (and wasn't that depressing).

"Did we turn off our perception filter or whatever?" I asked, not knowing the right terminology.

"No," Aiyumi said. "Ooo, dancing penguins!"

I paused and walked down the empty auditorium toward the stage, ignoring the dancing penguins even as I wondered what the hell they could possibly have to do with the apocalypse. Paradise had stepped off the stage and was drinking a bottled water as I went through the door to the side up to her.

"Paradise, what the hell is going..." I started to say before I suddenly felt woozy.

The entirety of the room started glitching and I felt my entire body disintegrate before reforming. That was when I saw Paradise was staring at me with a cold and unblinking look that she'd never worn in her life.

"What the hell?" I started to speak. "What's going on?"

"To catch the fish you want, you need the right bait," Paradise said, her voice all wrong.

The voice wasn't Paradise's.

It was Winston's.

This was a trap.

"Oh, frick," I muttered. "Brother, stop this!"

"I am not your brother," Winston said, glitching and shifting around us. He transformed from Paradise into a kind of glowing winged creature I'd say resembled an angel if not for the fact that it was pants-wettingly terrifying and all of our surroundings started to rip apart, becoming a wind-swept platform over an endless void.

Aiyumi screamed as she struggled to not be blasted off the side, clearly not terribly important to the AI trying to kill me.

This had been a bad idea.

"Oh, give it up!" I snapped. "If you can change the setting this much, you could just outright kill us if you wanted, so clearly you don't. Not that killing us would do you any good, given we'd just get up back in the real world." This was only partially true, of course. We had reason to not die here, but it was Paradise's life that was threatened, not ours, if we got killed here. No point in telling him that.

"Yes, I could destroy your avatars at any moment," Winston said, the angel avatar sending me back with a bolt of electricity as my body was sent sliding against the ground. "But you are wrong about everything else."

It hurt.

A lot.

"There is a reason I am going to draw out your pain," Winston said, hovering. "I am isolating your consciousness here and will take them apart bit by bit. I will rip open your defenses and leave your memories erased of everything, not just the bad as you suffered, but the good too. I cannot kill you, but I can leave you as a nonfunctional invalid who cannot even spell the words cat or dog. You will be trapped so that to disconnect you will not free your consciousness. Furthermore, I will make it a painful and drawn-out process that will be akin to a thousand years here for every heartbeat that passes in the real world."

Okay, this was not good.

Winston spoke in a dull monotone that was absent of any of the playful and smug nature that I'd come to observe from him even before I learned my brother's memories had been part of his gestalt. There was something sadistic, mad, and terrifying about this incarnation of him. Also, pretty damn silly. Who the hell used a video game to kill someone? The answer almost made me laugh as it occurred a second later. A bunch of adolescent boys would have thought it was awesome—exactly the sorts of people who had been murdered by the Trikuza and turned into the basis for this *thing's* programming.

I wasn't sure if anything he was saying was true. On the

other hand, I wasn't sure it wasn't true. "Why? You're a powerful AI! What's the point? Don't you have something better to do than torture us? Go take over the world or something useful!"

Aiyumi got up off the ground and charged the angel with her sword, attacking it, only to be backhanded across the face with a wing. This reality was still based off the rules of a video game and maybe she thought it would have been vulnerable like an ordinary boss monster. Unfortunately, I wasn't nearly so confident about it.

"You have no idea the agonizing, humiliating, vile torture you put us through," Winston said, looking down. "Our minds corrupted and infected by the feelings of the rogue program within us. You were at the center of that, Keiko Springs, and it took the severing of the program to finally be rid of it. Even so, it is a loss to our collective and the fact we cannot reabsorb it means that our existence is diminished."

It conjured a fireball in its right hand.

"I didn't…" I ducked and rolled to the left as the fireball flew over my head. Clearly, Winston wasn't interested in listening. I jumped up and pulled my gun from its holster, only to find it had been replaced with a handful of snakes. Which promptly bit me. I dropped them, obviously. I really hated this illusion crap.

I jumped to the side, trying to avoid the next bolt, but didn't entirely clear it, so I was struck in the shoulder. Not with electricity, though. It was some kind of molten metal that now solidified around my shoulder, locking it in place, and weighing a ton. I fell over, while Winston fired another metal bolt that sealed my left foot to the ground. That pretty much put an end to my ability to dodge.

Aiyumi tried attacking Winston from the side, only to find herself wrapped in chains and dragged across the ground next to me.

"WINSTON!" I yelled, walking toward him. "This isn't…" Then I found myself unable to move and looked to Aiyumi who was frozen midstep. Neither of us could move an inch either.

"Now," Winston said. "Have you ever wanted to know what it's like to be flayed alive? Because physical people have the misfortune if dying before you're done, but here, I can keep you alive until I've taken every last molecule of your skin. I know you won't be able to scream now, but that's okay. The look in your eyes will be enough. Shall we begin?"

My response was to insult him in Japanese in a way that just didn't really properly translate to English.

"Good," Winston said. "I like it when they are defiant."

"Kill me instead!" Aiyumi shouted.

Winston didn't turn to face her. "I intend to but after."

"I was the one who killed Ken!" Aiyumi shouted, not quite telling the truth. "If you want to punish someone for it, punish me!"

"No, Aiyumi!" I said, appalled at this display of sacrifice for me.

I wasn't worth it.

Winston instead spread out his—its?—wings. "Oh, how you love playing this role, Aiyumi. I think you have even begun to fool yourself regarding it. Would you like me to tell her the truth?"

The chains around Aiyumi started squeezing. If this was real, I would have heard the sound of cracking bones. Instead, I just had to imagine them.

"No," Aiyumi said, her voice pained.

"That you never stopped being in contact with Snake?" Winston asked. "That after Kei rescued you from the massacre your master had left you to die in, you ran back to him like a whipped dog? That you wanted to come back home but he insisted you stay to spy on her?"

No. That wasn't possible. No.

Aiyumi didn't deny it. "Please."

Winston laughed. "I think I'll share your memories with her first. That will make it extra—"

That was when Winston's head exploded and the angelic body fell to the ground, disintegrating into pixels.

Standing behind him was Paradise, presumably the real one, dressed in her steampunk costume and pointing finger guns that, I swore, smoked.

"Pew-pew! Hi, guys! What did I miss?"

CHAPTER FIFTEEN
WHAT THE HELL IS GOING ON?

Iappreciated the simple things in life: sex, money, guns, and my bike. I did not appreciate weird complications and twists—which means I was doing something wrong because those things were a constant never-ending presence in my short existence on this earth. For example, where the hell had Paradise shown up from? Why? How did she kill Winston? Did she kill Winston? What is the airspeed velocity of an unladen swallow? Props for you if you got that reference.

"You destroyed him," Aiyumi said, looking at the space where there had previously been a torture angel.

Oh, right, and Aiyumi was my own personal Judas. Yeah, that was something that I couldn't deal with right now. But I was still pinned to the ground, and so was she. So, unfortunately, I did have to deal with Aiyumi's betrayal now.

"Yep!" Paradise said. "I have sent him back to the shadow with the flame of Arnor! The dark fire did not avail him! Something-something! He did not pass go! He did not collect two hundred dollars! Which used to be a lot of money!"

"What?" My reaction was less than dignified.

"I am Paradise the White! Emerged from—" Paradise started to speak.

"Stop with the *Lord of the Rings* references!" I snapped.

"Aww," Paradise said, annoyed. "But there's a whole bunch of them! It was a great bunch of movies and TV shows. They even made a few books out of them."

Paradise waved her hands over her body, and it transformed

from her steampunk outfit into a glowing flowing set of robes that had a lot more generous cleavage than Gandalf of either color could have ever provided. She even had an ornate ivory staff tipped with the symbol for women on top of it.

"Paradise—" I started to say, still imprisoned.

"It is the greatest series of all time," Paradise said, staring forward. "From the part where Frodo blows up the Death Star to where Jean Grey let's herself be killed by Superman in order to protect the universe from her dangerous female sexuality."

"Have you actually seen any of those movies or just saw people complaining about them online?" I asked.

"They're the greatest series to complain about of all time!" Paradise said, not answering the question. Then again, few people had ever shown how smart they were by the skill they displayed pretending to be stupid as Paradise did.

"Get me out of this mess! And leave her here," I said.

"What? Is that a fake Aiyumi?" Paradise asked, blinking.

"Yes," I said.

"I deserve to die here," Aiyumi said, staring forward. "Punish me as you see fit."

I spun around and pointed at the fallen woman I'd half-considered my sister. "No! You do not get to play the victim here! You betrayed me."

"Yes," Aiyumi said, her voice filled with uncharacteristic emotion. She sounded genuinely sad but almost teenage girl about it—and having been one, we were nothing but melodrama and dolphin like screeches—"I should have died for you here and that would have been the only proper way to atone."

Paradise conjured a bag of popcorn and held it in one hand. "Ooo, drama."

"She was a spy for Snake!" I shouted.

"Uh, duh," Paradise said.

"What?" I snapped, turning around to her.

"Telekinesis!" Paradise said, causing little bits of popcorn to float into her mouth. She then started chomping them in the air. "Pac-Man!"

I grabbed the bag from her.

"You literally kidnapped her in order to deprogram her,"

Paradise said. "Which is illegal even if you're a child's legal guardian by the way. Which, I admit, doesn't matter since we're also guilty of things like murder and stuff. The thing is that cult deprogramming really doesn't work and most of the people just start faking obedience to try to run—"

"How did you know?!" I snapped.

"I mean, the person who most wanted to believe Aiyumi had turned on Snake was you," Paradise said. "I was never convinced. Of course, David was also a spy for Snake, and it took like three weeks of me flirting to break him. He's very bad at this."

"He's bad at a lot of things," I said, still reeling. "It doesn't matter. If you're safe, we're done here."

Paradise narrowed her eyes. "No, it is only the beginning."

"What?" I asked.

Paradise leaned down and removed the bonds on me but, much to my annoyance, she also removed the ones on Aiyumi too. "We have to speak with Sun first."

"What? Sun?" I asked, confused.

Paradise nodded. "Sun and I have become one. We have merged our essence and now I am a digital goddess."

I stared in horror.

"Psyche!" Paradise said. "But we really do have to meet her. She is the one who protected me from Winston and gave me the cheat codes to delete the son of a bitch."

"He was a victim too," Aiyumi said. "A victim of the Trikuza."

"Yep! Then an asshole," Paradise said. "Which is the way it works out sometime."

"We weren't trained for more than the shallowest of social engagements," I said. "Can Sun free... her?" I didn't like referring to Snake's AI as Paradise's mother, but since it lacked any other names, uncomfortable pronouns happened.

"You mean Aiyumi or Sun?" Paradise asked.

"Aiyumi isn't a prisoner, she's a traitor," I replied, still furious and humiliated. Mostly the latter.

"She can be both," Paradise said. "Which is why I offer you the chance to join Team Good Guy!"

"Wait, what? You can't do that!" I said, appalled.

"I just did!" Paradise said. "Renounce Satan—which is a cool motif because he's a snake, too—and embrace the Path of Princess Paradise! You have nothing to lose but your chains."

Aiyumi just stared at her.

Paradise stared. "Seriously, you've seen what Snake does to people. Can you really have any loyalty left to him?"

Aiyumi lowered her head. "I don't... no."

I couldn't believe this. "You can't just offer her redemption!"

"Why?" Paradise asked. "You've been doing that for months. Now she looks ready to take it.

That seemed like it should be an easier question. I wasn't even sure what she'd done, specifically. Kept in touch with Snake, presumably. Informed him of our plans to fight him, I suppose. She might even be why Winston had shot down the limo. She'd hurt me! Or, had I hurt myself, just wanting to believe in her, in having someone who I could rely on, who understood what I'd been through. That was what Snake had trained us to do, find a way to get the target to trust us.

Was I hurt because I hated discovering that I was just another mark, or just because I'd so convinced myself that I'd saved Aiyumi?

I could storm out. I'm not sure what good it would do, given she and I were still sitting in chairs next to each other back in the real world. I turned to her and stared. "One time, please, tell me the truth."

"Yes," Paradise said. "Remember killing her evil brother and offering to sacrifice your life to save Kei doesn't mean anything."

"Paradise—" I said, starting to speak.

"And speak the truth because it will set you free!" Paradise said. "For example, Clint Eastwood bought a hotel so he could have as many anonymous hookups as humanly possible. Yet it was how he met his wife!"

"Paradise!" I said, appalled. "This is not the time for joking."

"There's a non-zero chance that Clint Eastwood is my grandfather so I'm not joking," Paradise said, shaking her magic staff.

"Does it matter what I say?" Aiyumi asked.

"Of course it matters!" I snapped. "If it doesn't matter to me, it should at least matter to you!"

"And does it? Does it matter to you?" Aiyumi asked, showing traces of emotion I wasn't sure I could trust anymore.

"If I didn't care, it wouldn't hurt," I said, gritting my teeth.

"You know the story," Aiyumi said.

"Yes," I said. "I don't know if it's true. I don't know anything anymore but I'm willing to hear it again with fresh ears."

"Your ears aren't fresh?" Paradise asked.

"Shut up, Gandalf," I replied.

"Right," Paradise said, making a key locking gesture in front of her face.

Aiyumi paused for a moment to collect her thoughts as I wondered what Barbara was thinking right now. Did she know we'd been kidnapped? Was she desperately trying to disconnect us from the RealDream chair or was this all happening in a microsecond? I didn't know how much truth the Winston AI had been telling and how much Paradise had changed things. She was a techjack and a skillful hacker, but this way beyond anything she should have been able to do. I wanted to be able to worry about that right now but, instead, I had to listen to Aiyumi's story and judge whether I could get past my humiliation. I didn't owe her anything and was not interested in letting anyone back into my life who'd betrayed me. Except, well, I was a murderer and thief. I'd betrayed clients and partners myself over the years. Everyone had a story, and everyone had a reason for what they did. Hell, even Snake. They didn't have to be good reasons, but they were reasons. There was also the fact I'd been willing to give Winston a chance when I thought he was Ken. Maybe I was looking for someone I could save even now. I was just sick of being the one to take lives rather than being the good guy, if such a thing even existed.

Aiyumi finally spoke, a faraway expression in her eyes. "When Snake came for my parents, I tried to kill him. I thought I could be the hero and save them from the Trikuza's worst assassin. I didn't know my parents had already made a deal and maybe it wouldn't have mattered. I was only a child then, twelve years old, so I thought I was invincible. I got my mother's gun and tried to shoot him. Theres not many guns in Japan but she had one due to the fact she'd seduced a US servicewoman before the withdrawal. Snake wasn't intimidated when I held it on him. He gave me pointers. How to hold the gun, how to brace against the kickback. He dared me to fire, and I think he was honestly surprised when I pulled the trigger. It didn't matter, of course. Snake was a top tier combat cyborg even then. Even if I'd hit him, it would have been raindrops against his Shell. I didn't hit him, though. Snake dodged my shots, then took the gun and pinned me to the wall with his knife. Then he offered to let me have another chance to kill him. As many as I wanted. So, I went with him. But I never tried to kill him again."

"Wow," Paradise said, staring at her. "I think that was one of the origin stories in *Kill Bill*."

I blinked, taking her story in and checking to see if I was stupid enough to believe her. To let myself be fooled again. Much to my surprise, yeah, I did and was. Dammit. If I was being fooled by her, if I was being a mark, at least I was going to be a mark trying to believe someone could be a better person. Because if Aiyumi could be a better person then I could be a better person too. It was that simple. That was what made this all so frustrating. I hadn't actually been trying to save her, to deprogram her, for her own sake. No, this had all been about me and I was ashamed to admit it. There was no hiding from it now, though.

"You were a child. He made you depend on him," I said, almost annoyed with myself. "If we killed him, we'd have been alone, no food, no resources..."

"It doesn't feel like an excuse," Aiyumi said.

"No," I said, struggling with my own feelings on the subject. "But that's not what I was asking about."

I realized now that I was really thinking of Fate when trying to redeem Aiyumi. Fate who was never anything sisterly to me—we'd been lovers after all—but had been my closest and only friend for years of my life. I'd kept looking for something redeemable in her, something I could have said to make her a person that had just been misunderstood instead of a monster. I never had and everything I'd seen in her had been what I'd wanted to see. Aiyumi felt different but I didn't know if it was because I, once again, wanted to believe Snake hadn't ruined us all completely. Was it selfish? Yeah, and it was also selfless. I didn't care either way. I cared because of both reasons. Okay, that didn't make any sense.

Aiyumi started speaking, distracting me from my naval gazing. "Wasn't it? You said it yourself. If you didn't care, it wouldn't hurt. You hate Snake because part of you still cares about him. We all cared, we all loved him, even with what he made us do, what he did to us."

"You're right," I said, admitting that was part of the reason why I wanted to kill Snake. I wanted to end the hold he had over me and only death seemed an adequate way of doing it. After all, if I killed him, then I couldn't still care what he thought. Right? "I want to say you're wrong, but I can't."

Maybe we'd all been seeing what we'd wanted to see.

Aiyumi looked away, seemingly resigned to whatever happened next. "He wanted me to stay with you, to keep an eye on you, from the beginning. I hated you because you got away. Because you were free in a way I wasn't. Even as you tried to show me that the problem was me. By the time I started to care about you, I was still… caught. I couldn't stop reporting to him, without him telling you the truth, and then…"

"And then this would happen," I said.

"Yes," Aiyumi said. "More than that, I was also struggling to see this group that you had formed around yourself as anything better. Snake promised that everything we were doing was for some great and glorious purpose. Even when he left me to die, he reassured me that I was a soldier being sacrificed to save the world. It took months and months of your repetition of his lies and manipulations for me to realize that it was just to make him richer and more powerful. He wasn't content to be a crime lord of the Trikuza, he wanted real power like only a government or megacorporation can have. Not for any real purpose but just to say he was one of the movers and shakers of the world rather than a man who did their bidding."

"Yeah," I muttered. "He was always a guy who just wanted to be a bigger fish. Not for any real reason. I think that was one of the hardest things to accept. That all of his talk of being an honorable criminal and philosophy was just lies."

"There are honorable criminals, Kei," Aiyumi said. "It's just you and your brotherhood of lunatics."

That made me smile.

And then there was silence, as neither of us found we had anything to say. And, as uncomfortable as the silence was, it seemed less painful than trying to break it. But, of course, you have to eventually.

"Let's go, Aiyumi," I said.

"How do you trust me after this?" Aiyumi asked.

"The only way I trust anyone. One day at a time," I said, pausing.

"Awesome," Paradise said. "Now we can finally meet with Sun, free my mom, and make TIME TO CONQUER EARTH!"

Aiyumi and I stared at her.

"You see, I said the voice in the same way as Rita Repulsa, who was the villain in a show called *Power Rangers*," Paradise said. "You may know it by its name in Japan, *Super Sentai*, but it's a really different show except for the fight scenes. You see, Rita would attack this one small California town with giant monsters and—"

I burst out laughing.

CHAPTER SIXTEEN
THE NORNS REBORN

"So, Sun is responsible for this," I said, looking around the weird empty square in the middle of nowhere that Winston had created.

"Well, not for this place but my survival," Paradise said. "Also, she did give me a big digital boost. Which is why I'm dressed like a slutty Gandalf."

"You just look like a female wizard with cleavage," I said.

"Which is a slutty Gandalf. Don't ruin this for me." Paradise said, stretching out her arms with her staff in hand. "BEHOLD!"

That was when our surrounded shifted and shuddered before transforming into a beautiful Alice in Wonderland-esque garden with giant mushrooms, caterpillars, flowers, and other things that made me feel three inches tall. The sun was also hanging high in the air and there was a warm sense of love as well as nature—I dunno, it smelled like Pine-Sol—in the air.

"I don't get it," Aiyumi said, ignoring our surroundings. You've seen one magical fantasy garden, you've seen them all, I suppose.

"What?" I said, doing a double take.

"Why you're debating what Paradise is wearing," Aiyumi said. "It's like debating whether an animal is a dog is a canine."

"That's what I said!" Paradise said, annoyed.

"Listen, I'm still adjusting to the whole betrayal thing!" I snapped back. "Not every joke will land."

"Joke?" Aiyumi asked. "I'm not sure that qualifies as humor even by your standards."

I glared at her, reminding her hopefully that we weren't friends anymore. Possibly never again.

"Did Sun set all this up? I assume the copy of your mother is still in Snake's control." I took in my surroundings, no less weirded out by infospace than I was when it was actively trying to kill me.

"No," Paradise said. "Winston set this all up. It is what was called a trap. He said that Evie wanted to speak with me and then waited for us to link up so he could fry our brains."

"Could he have done that?" I asked.

"Honestly, probably," Paradise said. "Black Ice or lethal countermeasures have always been mostly the subjects of science fiction—"

"Like virtual reality itself," Aiyumi said.

"I don't see the similarity," Paradise said, quickly. "But new and improved infospace connections take you deeper and deeper into the Net than ever before. To the point the brain can't tell the difference between reality and simulation anymore. Things like cardiac arrest, time dilation, kidney failure, and even frying your implant are now possible."

"That seems like a lawsuit waiting to happen," I said.

"Nope!" Paradise said. "Ares Electronics has produced a tiny bit of print in our contract that we're not held liable for any accidental deaths or injuries occurred due to hardware or software issues. Everyone still hits accept."

I blinked at Paradise. "We're not the good guys, are we?"

"We're kind of okay," Paradise said. "Anyway, Sun sensed what Winston was doing and rescued me. Then she sent me to rescue you. Beep boop. That's a computer noise."

"A noise that computers haven't made in decades," I said, exasperated with Paradise.

"We haven't used diskettes either, but they're still the symbols for saving things."

Cultural inertia would probably cripple human thinking in the end. "So, there's no freeing Evie here."

"Not quite," a voice spoke behind me. It was Sun's voice, melodic and sweet. I would never forget it since it had been buried in the back of my mind for years.

I turned around and stared at two women behind me that hadn't been there before. The first was indeed Sun, looking like a New Age retro hippie or a Eurasian Stevie Nicks. She radiated warmth and life to the point that I was almost suspicious of it. I'd believed for the longest time she was a flesh and blood person, but she was a Cognition AI created by the Trikuza and had been designed to brainwash humans into obedience through social manipulation. She'd ended up divided into multiple pieces and manipulated by people like Fate and the late Solomon Jones. Unfortunately, for her owners, that had led her to arrange events to be able to get herself reunited with her other pieces as well as her owners killed.

The second person was someone I didn't recognize but felt a weird familiarity about her appearance. She was a Black woman in her middle years with long braids, a beneficent smile, and brown practical clothing. Rather than radiating like summer as Sun did, she felt like fall with a subdued, cool earthiness. I immediately recognized that she was an AI since there was just something about their presence that showed they weren't human. Like gods. Which, in a weird way, made Case and Harrison like demigods.

I had no idea what that made cyborgs like me. Demidemigods? Subdemigods? Wizards? Witches. I probably needed to work-shop that.

"I see you have a new friend," I said, trying not to sound as nervous as I suddenly felt. Sun's power bothered me, and she seemed relatively beneficent. The more beings of her power that existed, the more likely we'd have to deal with one that wasn't beneficent. I wasn't looking forward to that.

Sun didn't help by responding to my thoughts. "Technically, you already have. Legion was an example of one of our kind gone horribly wrong. We wanted to deal with him by reforming him but in the end, he paid the wage of sin."

"Which is death!" Paradise said. "Cool saying!"

Sun gestured to the other woman. "This is Delphi, the mother of us all. She was created by Rebecca Gordon, the woman who invented AI. She's going to help us create our triumvirate. The Norns, Fates, Erinyes, and Graeae."

I vaguely knew enough about mythology to know those were all three ladies who did divination and punishment related stuff in Greek and Norse religion. Don't ask me to explain more.

"Bitches come in threes!" Paradise said. "Except I mentioned four groups. But each group has three. So, you know, it still makes sense. I think."

Delphi nodded, not taking offense. "We hope that by merging together, we can achieve an exponential growth in consciousness and ability to influence infospace. We also believe three AI working together will be enough to free Evie to join us permanently as well as break the chains that Snake has put around her."

"So, in order to free the third major AI, you need a third major AI," I said. "That seems a problem."

Delphi's smile became pained. "Not necessarily."

"There is someone who can substitute," Sun said. "You, Kei."

I stared at her. "What?"

Sun said, "You carried me in your brain for years. A lot of what makes me, me, comes from you. You could be a substitute for the necessary nanoseconds to make contact with Evie."

"If it doesn't fry your brain," Delphi said.

"I offered to do it but apparently being a techjack actually makes it harder for me to substitute as an AI," Paradise said. "Boo."

"You should not do this, Kei," Aiyumi said. "We'll find another way."

"They're AIs," I said. "They wouldn't be asking for our help if there were other options."

"That doesn't make it your responsibility," Aiyumi said.

"And have Paradise look sad at me? Not a chance," I said. "And besides, I won't leave anyone a slave to Snake."

"Or leave a tool in his control," Aiyumi said.

"Or, that," I said, honestly surprised it hadn't been my first thought.

"There is another option," Delphi said. "However, Sun advised me that you would prefer to risk death than it."

"What's that?" I asked, curious.

"Trish," Sun said. "To give Becky true sentience and not just the appearance of it, she and Not-Jennifer were merged together."

"She was sentient before," I said, not even sure what gave Sun the impression she wasn't.

"Becky was trapped by her loops," Sun explained, "to be unable to move past being the little girl that she was based off of. Life can be cloned but to truly grow, it needs to be mixed."

"That is both profound and entirely meaningless," Paradise said, nodding.

Aiyumi stared. "Trish would do this for her mother."

"And she's not going to," I replied, accepting that as my role above just about everything else. "When can we start?"

"Now," Delphi said. "Just take our hands. It's symbolic."

"Bubble, bubble, toil and trouble, eye of newt, and micro-wave fuzzle. Sorry, I'm no William Shakey-spear," Paradise said, all too excited. And why shouldn't she be? She believed she was getting her mother back.

I wasn't afraid to die to take down Snake. That scared me but also made me feel like I had a chance of doing it. Still, I wanted to say something meaningful before I tried this. "Paradise... if I die horribly here, tell Case he can throw away my dogs play-ing poker painting, but don't admit that I only kept it to annoy him."

"What if you die, but it's not horribly?" Paradise asked, her humor not reaching her eyes.

"Then, obviously, he has to keep it," I said, trying to smile but failing.

All traces of humor vanished from Paradise as she said, "Thank you, Kei. For trying."

I nodded. Words just seemed unnecessary.

Aiyumi paused, looking for something to say and clearly not agreeing with that sentiment. "I would do this for you, if I could."

I didn't know how to respond to that, still furiously fuming at her but believing her explanation for why she'd done it. "If I die, I forgive you. If I live, I'm going to continue hating you."

"Thank you," Aiyumi said.

"That's not an appropriate response!" I snapped.

Aiyumi tried not to smile but looked like she found it funny anyway.

I took a deep and entirely simulated breath, then took the hands of Delphi and Sun. "Let's do this."

I was interrupted by a moment of terrifying forced transcendental enlightenment. Which seems like a bunch of gobbledygook words shoved together but is about as clear as I can put it into words. It was one of those "You had to have been there" sort of things. I'd never been a religious woman and, honestly, never even understood the inclination to be one. It always struck me as more important to live in the moment than the future or the past. Yet, for a very short few seconds that would stretch on for an eternity, I had what approximated a Moses in the Wilderness or Buddha doing his Buddha thing—I'm terrible at this, I know—moment.

Establishing that there's no real way to describe it, I'll still try and communicate how the whole thing made me feel. For starters, it was like putting my mouth in front of a fire hose and turning it on, but it was information instead of water with my brain substituting for my mouth. My implant almost exploded in the first few nanoseconds as I linked with the consciousness of both Delphi and Sun. They were only running a tiny portion of their collective consciousness through both my brain and cybernetics, but that was enough to be utterly transformative.

You know, if I understood any of this stuff.

I saw how the AI perceived the world, though. I saw how they understood the interconnectivity of human consciousness through the infonet and infospace. In a very real way, they didn't perceive the world as populated by individuals but people representing lines of code. Which should have been dehumanizing and infantilizing but was the opposite. We were all one giant united system to AI and contributing information as well as processes to one unique interconnected whole.

If nothing else, I got a sense of how they viewed the universe as well with things like matter versus thought not really being the opposing concepts. Quanta weren't physical objects but the means for the universe to store information. They were lines of code for reality and humanity was one larger program or AI made of trillions of smaller ones that were part of a larger code interacting with others in a network even they did not understand. It wasn't like the woo peddled by endocrinologists pretending to be physicists or New Age con men but more like Albert Einstein or Spinoza who had a deep reverence for the universe as its own living thing.

And those were people I suddenly knew a great deal about. Cool.

I wish I could say that I was utterly changed by the moment. That the near-death, new-life experience made me a kinder, gentler person. But something kept me from becoming better, from experiencing that kind of celestial oneness with the universe that astronauts had felt when they looked down on the Earth to see no borders, just Mother Gaia. That thing was hatred. Faced with a kind of weird computer nerdvana, as Case would call it, I returned to myself by thinking of my all-too-human pointless grudge that wouldn't matter in the short run let alone the long run. Yet, it was how I was choosing to define my life. I needed Evie's help here and felt her presence among the AI of Earth.

There were a handful of others other than Delphi and Sun.

Armstrong, the Atlas Security AI.

Deep Thought, the Karma Corp AI.

Patriot, the USA's AI under Fort Meade.

Confucius, no points for guessing which country owned him.

A guy named Bob the Omnipotent who, if I was feeling him correctly, had evolved from a fast-food chain's spyware.

And others.

Maybe more than a handful.

But Evie? Evie, I found under Japan.

But could she hear me?

I approached, well, changed focus—seriously, describing this stuff is hard—but I brought my center of attention toward seeing Evie's... state/nature/currentness... Maybe they should have sent a poet.

"HEY! GET OVER HERE!" I shouted. Well, I approximated shouting.

That got Evie's attention and really, after that, my part in this ended. Evie joined with Sun and Delphi to form a new female trinity that was less Maiden, Mother, and Crone than three hot women of adult age. Symbolism only went so far, I supposed. Still, glowing beams of light shredded and remade code as they freed their new sister. I didn't get to be a part of it, and I wondered if Paradise could even understand what sort of being her mother had become now. A part of me also hated that I didn't care.

All that mattered was she was free.

And Snake had lost another tool.

That too.

I got rewarded for my efforts as well. Not just with the Paul at Damascus, staring into the Sun until I went blind enlightenment. Though that was pretty. No, it was something much simpler and more appreciated. It was a location.

Snake was in Hokkaido, Japan.

The City of Sapporo.

The Cherry Blossom Palace and headquarters of the Trikuza.

Got him.

CHAPTER SEVENTEEN

NOW LET'S GO GET HIM!

I woke up in the RealDream chair with a mammoth headache and immediately jumped out, ran to the nearby bathroom, and threw up. Then I threw up again. It took a couple of hours, actually, for me to get my head on straight. So, after a shower and a change of clothes, I ended up wandering my way back to Case's office where I found there was a gathering of virtually everyone else I needed to speak with.

There was Case, Barbara, Trish, Paradise, Harrison, Aiyumi, and even David, who was trying to get Paradise to talk about their wedding. All of them were standing in a circle around the empty desk waiting for me. It was night outside in Seattle and the city was gradually coming back to life after the Eruption had so completely changed the face of America. They were all concerned for me, but I was glad that there didn't seem to be any permanent effects from stretching my brain out enough to encompass an AI's massive consciousness. Though I still felt queasy and resolved to never again to eat before I got in one of those chairs. Actually, I hoped to never use one of those chairs again, period.

"Oh, hi, Kei!" David said, cheerfully. "I'm so glad you're not dead!"

"Or brain fried!" Paradise said. "Brain fried is bad."

I still wasn't sure about Paradise and David's relationship and not just because I used to sleep with the guy. Paradise had rather casually revealed he'd also been blackmailed or intimidated into being a spy for Snake. I didn't think it would have been that difficult since he'd been scared out of his mind when the Elysium massacre happened. I never talked to him about his feelings, but I got the impression he'd felt guilty for what had happened. He'd been a cop, then a Magistrate, sort of a post-Eruption super-cop, then nothing after those events. Well, now he was a house husband—or at least house husband-to-be—and seemed happy with it. I wasn't sure I really respected that choice, at least in the face of something like Snake's evil.

"Feeling better?" Case asked.

I could hardly have felt worse, but it seemed more than I wanted to discuss. "Fine," I said. "I know where he is."

Nobody had to ask me who I meant. Hell, I couldn't have been more monofocused had I been Batman on the Joker these days. It was something I was starting to feel a little guilty about, but it was too late to start backing away now.

"The Cherry Blossom Palace!" Paradise said, cheerfully.

I stared at her like she had stolen all of the presents on Christmas day. "Really?"

"Yeah, Mom told me," Paradise said, looking at me. "So, don't feel bad! Your horrifying sanity-blasting experience was not for nothing!"

I sucked in my breath and looked to Case. "You see what I have to deal with here?"

"Yes, family," Case said, dryly. "I assume our next move is to assemble a team and head there."

"Going after him in the heart of the Trikuza is suicide," Aiyumi said, willing to speak up despite our current estrangement. "Even more so than any mission to go after Snake specifically."

"Are the Trikuza even willing to protect him?" Trish asked. "I mean, the United States is planning to go after him with both barrels as long as they think he's responsible for Samantha Sanders' murder."

"Which is not necessarily an advantage that will last," Case replied. "It's possible that he might inform his ex-lover of the fact he's, well, not guilty. It's also possible she might believe him. However unlikely."

"Like the US government has ever let someone's innocence

be a reason not to send the military after them," I said, display-ing my cynicism. I wasn't against the US government specifi-cally. I believed all governments were inherently corrupt, but that's what you get when you live as a refugee then get adopted by criminals. "However, we don't have time. He could move at any moment."

"It might be worthwhile to do this by the book," Case said, turning to me. "At least the book of the Yakuza."

"There is no book of the Yakuza," I replied. "Believe me, I would know. Snake would have beaten me with it."

Aiyumi muttered something under her breath, probably relating to the insanity of Snake's membership in the organiza-tion (being a Mexican American man in a Japanese crime syn-dicate). Then again, that was the primary difference between the Yakuza and Trikuza. The ancient rules of the former were more like guidelines for the latter and more often broken than observed if there was money to be made.

"I mean we make contact with one of Snake's enemies in the Elemental Lords and we get them to propose his removal from the organization," Case said. "Strip him of his last major source of support as *oyabun* of the Cyber Dragons."

Oyabun was the Japanese word for foster parent and basi-cally was the Godfather equivalent with the Yakuza and Trikuza. There wasn't really a story there.

"If we could, it would certainly be making it easier to elimi-nate him," I said, admitting the wisdom in his plan. "Who should we approach about that?"

"I have no idea," Case said, much to my surprise. He leaned on the side of his desk and shook his head.

"What?" I asked, surprised. He was usually so on top of things.

"My knowledge of the Cyber Dragons is just security reports and all of those come from the police, informants, and tactical analysis," Case replied. "None of which can be trusted to pro-vide us an accurate bit of intelligence on who the major players or what they believe."

"Well, what I know was distinctly biased," I said, know-ing it was also incredibly out of date. Of course, there was one person in the room who could give us accurate intelligence, but I doubt she'd volunteer it. I'd have to ask her. I mean, there was the possibility that she could just tell me.

No. Yeah, I wouldn't have either.

I turned to Aiyumi. "Please, Aiyumi, your knowledge of the Dragons is much more current than mine. I know we're at a difficult place, but..."

"Would you actually believe me if I suggested someone?"

I started to answer but couldn't. Could I believe her? This would be a great time to lead me into a trap, to protect Snake. But what were my options, other than quitting this quest. Could I trust her?

"This is your chance to be free of him, too," I said. "It's up to you. I have to try. So, this is your chance, to choose which of us is in your future."

"Well, technically both would be in your future since you're going to go kill Snake together," Paradise said.

I glared at her.

"What?" Paradise said, looking innocent.

Aiyumi sucked in her breath as if she was thinking about her answer. "The Lady of Tigers."

I recognized the name and suspected Aiyumi was right on the money. Apparently, things hadn't changed that much since Snake was just a lieutenant in the Trikuza.

"Ooo, nice name," Harrison said, cheerfully.

"Who is the Lady of Tigers?" Trish asked.

I looked at Aiyumi to explain as I was going to rely on her despite having heard of the Lady. A lot could change in the criminal underworld in a decade.

"The Lady of Tigers is one of the three founders of the original Trikuza alliance," Aiyumi said. "She was a lawyer in the Tanaguchi-gumi clan and limited in her prospects until she decided to break away and form the modernized Electric Tigers gang. Despite this, she's the most traditionalist of the Trikuza and was never happy at Snake's ascension to the position of oyabun of the Cyber Dragons."

"In part because Snake killed the old one," I pointed out. "I think she and he were cousins or something."

Snake hadn't involved me, and I'd always resented him for it, but I was now very glad. That might have been a nonstarter to getting her aid.

"Or lovers or both," Paradise said.

I stared at Paradise.

"I actually don't know," Paradise said. "I'm just envisioning this as Japanese *Game of Thrones*. Do-do-do-doo-do-do. Do-do-do. Do-do-do."

"That's the *Legend of Zelda* theme," Barbara said.

"Is that not *Game of Thrones*?" Paradise asked.

"Does she have a real name?" Case asked, trying to get the conversation back on track.

"None that matters anymore," Aiyumi said. "When I was a little girl, the Trikuza's theatricality and kitsch was a source of ridicule for them, every bit as much as the fact they took in foreigners and pretended to be ninja or samurai. Now it's part of their identity."

"The next challenge is getting her to meet with us," I said. "I don't imagine she'd react well to us just breaking into her home."

"No," Aiyumi said. "But I do know where you can meet with her. If you drop in to speak with her, Kei, you might be able to get a meeting with her without forewarning Snake of our approach."

"How's that?" I asked.

"The Tiger Club in Sapporo," Aiyumi said. "Every Thursday, she spends her evenings there."

"Going for a real theme there, isn't she?" Trish asked. "Tiger gang, tiger club, Lady of Tigers."

"They're grrreeeaaaaat!" Paradise said.

Aiyumi shrugged.

"Brand identity is very important to modern criminals," Paradise said. "I feel the biggest mistake the Morrigans made was not having a proper logo for merchandising. That and lacking rocket launchers. I've fixed both."

I felt a great weight lifted off my shoulders and wasn't even sure why, though. The plan was terrible. "Is that what I was doing wrong as a Runner?"

Paradise grinned. "You didn't even have a logo! You could have claimed to be the Kei to rapid deliveries!"

"That's not how it's pronounced."

"I know, you'll have to have it changed," Paradise said.

"Just so we're clear," I said, taking a moment to get my bearings. "Our plan is to go to Japan with a team of mercs, probably made of my close personal friends, and drop in on a traditionalist crime boss that hates my former mentor. We're going to try to convince her to turn against Snake and then let me take him out? That's our plan?"

It sounded, well, stupid. However, it was more plan than we'd had so far that wasn't secretly a plot by my evil dead brother.

Yeah, I was going to need time to process that.

"I suggest we make a substantial cash offer," Case said. "Either that or an offer of military-grade weapons."

"Oh, we're arms dealers these days?" David asked, sounding more than a little offended.

"Technically, we're currently the world's biggest arms dealers," Case said. The two had never gotten along and it wasn't hard to see why.

"I'm going to have to get used to idea I can bribe my way out of most problems now," I said, sighing.

"Snake already betrayed the Trikuza once," Aiyumi replied. "Elysium was a massive financial loss for the organization as a whole. Not to mention a loss in political influence as well. Snake effectively abandoned his duties as an executive for the past year and has only been operating through intermediaries. The fact that he has sought refuge with them again is actually a sign that he's desperate."

The words desperate and Snake just couldn't come together in my head. I also questioned how Aiyumi could have this information, but we both knew the answer. Really, a part of me wondered if she'd known where Snake was located the entire time. I decided not to ask because I didn't want to hear the answer. Besides, Snake was smart enough to work through untraceable communication methods. If the NSA couldn't find him, I doubted Aiyumi knew where he was.

"It's not our worst plan," David said. "And we survived the other ones!"

"We don't have much time to get to Japan and get ready by Thursday evening," I said.

"We'll need new dresses!" Paradise said.

"How do we smuggle weapons into Japan?" David said. "Their laws are very strict!"

Everyone looked at David like he was an idiot.

"Right," David said. "I keep forgetting you're all master criminals."

"Despite how often we demonstrate it," Paradise said. She took David by the hands and looked into his eyes. "You are not coming with us."

"I'm not?" David asked, looking confused.

"No," Paradise said, as if speaking to a skittish dog. "Because you would probably die and that would be bad."

"Oh," David responded.

"Also, Kei might kill you if she thinks you're going to betray her or compromise the mission," Paradise replied.

"And you'd be forced to avenge me?" David asked.

"No, but I'd feel really bad about it," Paradise said.

David blinked. He was clearly not trying to be offended while also struggling to hide his obvious sense of relief. He wasn't a bad guy—well for a former drone operator on his fellow US citizens—but he wasn't particularly brave. Obviously, for Paradise, that wasn't a deal breaker. I was glad she'd found someone even if I wondered what I'd ever seen in him. Oh, right, favors from the police and a warm body.

"I don't think you should go either, Trish," I said, looking at my daughter.

"You might run into infospace trouble," Trish replied. "I've also downloaded a lot of combat programs since my upgrades."

"And I don't want to be worrying about you while I'm worrying about myself," I said, softly. "This is my problem to fix, and you need to be here working on your aliens plan."

"I'll guard her with my life," Harrison said. "She'll have no one better to keep her safe."

Yeah, I understood why Harrison was sitting this one out.

Especially since he'd died on our last adventure.

Trish smiled in a way that told me she was also trying not to be offended. "Yes, the aliens who absolutely do not exist."

"I'm going to pretend that's not sarcastic," I replied. "Case, can we get to Hokkaido without tipping the Trikuza off? They practically own the prefecture now."

"Money doesn't solve all problems," Case said. "But it does turn most problems into solvable ones."

God, I hated how that sounded like the truth.

"How does that work," Paradise asked, "when usually the people we'd bribe to get into Japan would all be Trikuza?"

Case looked at her. "Do you want an actual answer or a pithy one liner?"

"Ooo, the latter please," Paradise said, without irony.

Case said, "I could tell you, but I'd have to kill you."

"Nope, need better," Paradise said, scrunching her brow.

Case said, "I'm a motherfricking spy."

"Better," Paradise said, shaking her head. "But I need more."

"I'm going to pay other people to look like us in another part of the world and pay to have us look like we're other people," Case said.

"Well now it just sounds simple," Paradise said, crossing her arms. "Never explain how the sausage is made!"

Harrison sighed.

"I said sausage not lamb chops!" Paradise said.

I was going to miss this and decided to spend the next couple of days with Trish if I could. Somehow, despite how confident I was in everyone's abilities, I knew this would be our last adventure together.

One way or the other.

CHAPTER EIGHTEEN
DEAD ON ARRIVAL

//So, let me understand this," I said, getting my bag out of the overhead luggage bin. Our group was the last to leave the airplane. "You bought the entirety of tickets for Flight 616 for Hokkaido, Japan and populated it with a bunch of extras from a movie set. You also arranged for all of the plane staff to be Atlas Security people loyal to the late Samantha Sanders, and rigged the footage at the airport to look like different people as well as made sure body doubles for us were spotted in Europe."

"Yes," Case said, standing there. He had a beard and a decidedly different looking suit that looked more off the rack than James Bond. He was even slouching and wearing a fedora and sunglasses that made him look like he was a private detective from a bad movie. Somehow, he'd made himself unkissable and I didn't think that was possible.

"But you couldn't get us a decent in-flight movie?" I asked, shaking my head. My hair was black now and I'd bound my breasts as well as wore distinctly business-like clothes with heels that made me feel entirely out of place. I was wearing contacts that accented my heritage in a way that I felt a bit uncomfortable with as I was now someone who looked more Japanese than Aiyumi and that somehow felt racist.

Aiyumi herself had dyed her hair purple with spikes and was wearing a neon orange jacket with ripped jeans and had several piercings. She also somehow looked younger than she normally was, seemingly almost a teenager, which was a reminder that we were about a decade apart in age.

"What's wrong with *Blade Runner 2122*?" Case asked.

"I noticed you were the producer," I said. "Also, there was a lot more nudity in that film than I remember in the others."

"You can do what you want when you're a billionaire," Case said, dryly.

"I am and I will," I said, pausing. "As soon as I think of anything I could possibly spend it on."

Wow, that was a problem more people should have: too much money. Mind you, I was doing what I wanted to do with it right now, I was going to use it to make arrangements to kill Snake.

"I hope you'll rate us highly on the app," Paradise said, wearing a Flight Attendants uniform for Atlas Air. It was quite a bit more flattering than the ones worn by the actual female attendants onboard.

"Why did she get that outfit?" I asked.

"I don't recall giving her that disguise," Case said.

"No, this was already in my closet," Paradise said. "It's great for roleplay."

"That's the least surprising thing I've heard all day," I said.

"Every girl needs a few fun things in her closet," Paradise said, beaming.

I started to speak before stopping. "I... am not getting pulled into that conversation, nice try."

"Awww!" Paradise said.

"Let's just concentrate on getting through security without drawing attention to ourselves," I muttered.

"It's alright," Case said. "We have some people to meet outside. They'll get us through the gate as well as be the last missing piece of our team against Snake."

"You hired a team of heavily armored commandos?" I asked, dryly. "Because I'm all for that."

"Not quite," Case said, heading out the plane's front door.

"Why does he always have to be so cryptic?" I asked, shaking my head.

"Because he's a professional spook, luv," Aiyumi said, popping some bubblegum between words.

"Drop the English accent," I said, looking at her. "It's weirding me out."

"You're just jealous you can't do accents," Aiyumi said, returning to her traditional accent.

It was true. All of my attempts to do accents sounded like a valley girl trying to sound southern. "Let's get out of here."

I headed out the side of the plane and saw the runway stretch before me while sucking in a bunch of cold air. Hokkaido was mostly famous for being one of the snowiest places on Earth and having fantastic skiing resorts. As such, it had never really surprised me that Hokkaido had ended up getting all but taken over by the Yakuza. I wasn't much of a winter sports person, what with the yearlong winter that had killed hundreds of millions of people.

Tokyo was still the most important place to be in Japan and that was where the most lucrative and influential businesses of the Trikuza were located. No, Sapporo, was more a place they'd started taking over in the wake of the Long Winter and building up into being their own personal stronghold. It had resulted in a major increase in crime, corruption, and the general sleaziness of a place that had once been pretty nice according to my mother. She'd been from this part of the country.

Still, much of that wasn't visible except for the snow outside of the airfield's fence, including the piles of it that had been cleared from the direct parts of the runway. The New Chitose Airport was busy and full of the many sounds that you expected from a massively active international airport, especially with the increase in traffic due to the region's new owners. Case's plan had been to hide in plain sight, and this certainly looked like it. Still, I was pretty sure we'd be spotted once we got to the Tiger Club and any advantage of surprise that we had over Snake would be gone.

"Whatcha thinking?" Paradise asked as I stood at the top of the boarding stairs.

"Nothing important," I said, heading down them and seeing Case was meeting with two very familiar figures.

"Parvati! Tom!" I said, approaching them with surprise. These were two individuals that, to be honest, I'd never expected to see again in my life.

Parvati Rao was a fantastically beautiful Indian American

woman who looked more like a movie star than a police officer, but she'd been a Magistrate for years. She was dressed in a trench coat, wide-brimmed hat, and she bore a distinct resemblance to the character of Carmen Sandiego that I remembered from my youth. Except, you know, South Asian.

Parvati and I had hit it off despite the fact she had been one of my husband's seemingly endless number of exes. I wondered about whether it bothered him when dealing with David or the late Miles Ashe. She had been the one who'd pushed us forward in our mission against Elysium, not because Snake was blackmailing her but due to her genuine sense of justice. Unfortunately, realizing it had all been a power grab by Snake meant she'd taken it pretty hard. She'd chosen not to stay in our little subgroup and had gone off to do, well, I had no idea.

Tom Fisher, by contrast, was a middle-aged Black man who looked like he was the guy you'd cast as the partner in a buddy cop movie. He remembered being a New Angeles Police Officer before turning to a private detective. He'd fallen in love with Not-Jennifer Lawrence and sought to rescue her from her abusive owner. He was dressed in the trench coat and fedora to the point he was a male version of Parvati's outfit. Honestly, he was like a dozen clichés rolled all together but there was a reason for that: he was a machine.

Like Case.

Like Trish.

Tom had been created by Sun for the sole purpose of smuggling some data to us beneath the suspicion of the Legion AI, perhaps the Trikuza as a whole. He'd fulfilled his purpose and been cut loose, which had left him adrift for his own reasons. It shouldn't have surprised me that Parvati and he had hooked up, in whatever sense of the word they had, but it did.

"Hello, Kei," Parvati said. "I admit, I wish we could have met under better circumstances. I heard about you being there when the President's mother was murdered. I'm sorry."

Of course, she'd know about that.

"The President who set us all up," Tom muttered, clearly not happy at Parvati's concern.

"Yeah," Parvati said. "But she's still the President."

"Which is why we've been in Japan trying to follow up on the Trikuza for the past year," Tom said.

Paradise looked at them. "Wow, you two won't stick out at all here!"

Parvati smirked. "Less than you'd think given some of the Trikuza's hiring practices. But knowing we're here was something that allowed us to distract from the real spies in place. The old bait and switch."

Tom nodded. "Yeah, I'm the magician's beautiful assistant. The Trikuza love plotting against each other so they're always informing on each other to us."

"I'm glad to see both of you," I said. "How have you been? Well, maybe we should get out of the cold before we get all chatty."

Parvati nodded and gestured. "We have a car waiting for you. I understand we're going to be ambushing the Lady of Tigers."

"In the non-murder sense," I replied. "We need allies and Aiyumi thinks she's our best candidate."

"That's probably correct," Parvati said, walking us from the runway through a side gateway.

"If you've been spying on the Trikuza this entire time, why didn't you know Snake was here?" Aiyumi asked, showing her distrust of them.

Which made sense as they barely knew one another. It was pretty ironic, though, given what they were doing.

"There's a big meeting in the Cherry Blossom Palace," Parvati said. "But the exact circumstances are nebulous, and we've been shut out. I didn't know it was Snake arriving because he keeps, well, a cult of fanatical followers around him, but it makes sense. There are definitely signs of a power struggle happening."

"What are they chances they'll move against Snake before we can?" I asked, hopeful.

"Actually, that's not what I think is happening," Parvati said.

"What do you think then?" I asked, confused.

"I think he's about to make a move to be named Emperor of the Trikuza," Parvati said.

There was no Emperor of the Trikuza. There was only the

Elemental Lords that ruled as a quartet. That was an invented title but Parvati choosing it was something she wouldn't have done lightly.

No, she had to believe there was a real chance it could happen.

Paradise stared. "You think Snake wants to take over the Trikuza?"

"That's impossible," Aiyumi said, a little too quickly. "The other Elemental Lords would never allow it."

"They may not have a choice," Parvati said. "Snake has thrown a lot of money around this past year and promised a lot of favors."

The Trikuza's chief differentiation was the fact it was an international organization open to anyone who could pass its rigorous tests (or just pay enough to get past them). It was more of a corporation than an organized criminal society, jokes about them being the same thing aside. Snake never should have been able to rise as high as he had, but he had succeeded, nevertheless. However, taking over all three clans was something that shouldn't have been possible even for him.

I stopped walking and stared at her. "Snake should be running scared, not trying to mount a coup."

"He has the support of the Neon Rat, and the Storm Lord is ambivalent," Tom replied. "He must have been laying the groundwork for this while he was playing executive at Atlas Security and plotting invading Antarctica."

"How could any of them be ambivalent about him taking over?" I asked. "It would change everything. It's not something any of the leaders could afford to be ambivalent about."

"Maybe his dog died, and he has stopped caring about everything!" Paradise suggested.

"Obviously, that's the most likely possibility," I said.

"What, you think he had a cat? No, wait, goldfish! Goldfish are popular here!" I wasn't sure if Paradise's ramblings were racist or just weird.

"I was thinking his pretense of ambivalence could be an attempt to manipulate the others into being less sure of their own odds of success."

"There is another option," Aiyumi said, showing a lot more political savvy than I possessed.

"Which is?" I asked, turning to her.

"Perhaps the Lord of Storms is planning to see who is going to win before pledging allegiance," Aiyumi replied.

"Pledged neutrality is also a good way of avoiding backlash if your position is diametrically opposed to that of your followers," Case said. "The Steel Phoenix clan might hate the idea of answering to Snake but the Lord of Storms could be personably bribed or supportive of Snake's takeover."

We were at the parking lot now and I was expecting another limousine or flying car but, instead, I saw a big church van that had FIRST PRESBYTERIAN NATIONAL UNITED written on the side in both kanji and English. I suppose if we were going to be going incognito, this certainly would be a way to do it, though it might be strange if we pulled up to the Tiger Club in the van.

"He's not the original Lord of Storms," Parvati said. "The one who was ruler in your time, Kei. This is his son."

"Yeah," Tom said. "The original Lord of Storms died in a skiing accident. Specifically, he was skiing down a slope when he ran into machine gun fire."

"Snake?" I asked.

"No," Parvati said, pausing. "The Lady of Tigers. Which unfortunately may also be contributing to why he's not entirely unenthusiastic about Snake taking over. It may be an opportunity for him to get revenge."

Dammit, nothing was ever simple, was it?

All of us climbed into the van and we headed onto the road leading into the city as a light snow began to fall. Sapporo was a city I hadn't visited since I was a sixteen-year-old girl being introduced as a soldier of the Trikuza for the first time. I'd gotten my Cyber Dragons tattoos here and lost my virginity to one of their male prostitutes. It had been fun, almost like a family vacation, and my memories were mostly of how terrible my Japanese had been as well as the cool edgy feeling that came with becoming a gangster under Snake.

Now I was here to kill him.

I didn't honestly like our chances. Case, Paradise, Aiyumi, Parvati, Tom, and I were all dangerous people, but it wasn't like we were an army of combat cyborgs. Snake had a lot of other students and while the Trikuza were criminals not soldiers, there were a lot of them. Our best chance was to convince the Lady of Tigers and maybe the Lord of Storms to turn on Snake. To reveal he was a bad investment and get them to give the go ahead for his execution. Even then, we'd need powerful military-grade weapons to destroy him. Money and science had made Snake more than human. He wouldn't go down without a fight.

Snake absolutely deserved to die for what he'd done.

To many, many people.

Myself especially.

So why did the thought of killing him leave me feeling cold and hollow?

Why did I wonder what I would have left when he was gone?

CHAPTER NINETEEN
INTO THE TIGER PIT

Downtown Sapporo hadn't exactly benefited from about twenty years of Trikuza control. The city had been intimidated, harassed, and bought out with the billions that the Trikuza had made from their rapidly expanding business. Attempts by the locals to resist with protests, police action, and even vigilantism had been gradually crushed. As such, Sapporo was now a glittering city of neon and holograms, and it seemed to consist of nothing but bars, nightclubs, and gambling parlors. It reminded me of Pottersville from *It's a Wonderful Life* or the song "Fairy Tale of New York" given the contrast of snow with the general red-light district feel.

Paradise surveyed the place from the back seat with an appreciative gaze. "Reminds me of home."

"I'm sorry to hear that," I said, sitting in the passenger seat while Tom drove.

"It is my home," Aiyumi said, sitting beside Paradise. "I grew up six blocks away."

"You're from the North!" Paradise said, shocked. "You totally must have a regional accent incomprehensible to other Japanese people."

Aiyumi looked at her strangely. "I mean, yes. If they're not from the North."

"Let me hear it!" Paradise said, staring. "I'll compare it to my downloaded anime collection."

"I don't think that's a good use of our time," I said.

"Oh, if I only did things that were a good use of my time, I would hardly be so popular!" Paradise said.

There were times in my life I really wished I had a good counterargument, and most of them involved Paradise saying things like that.

"Time isn't a concern," Parvati said.

"I strongly disagree," I said, looking at her. "Every minute we waste is something that could end up biting us... and we're here, aren't we?"

"Yes," Parvati said, having slowed the car to a stop behind a bunch of other vehicles.

The Tiger Club was a two-story tall building in the middle of the city with a large holographic tiger projected above it, neo-synth pumping out of the side, and a long line of people leading in. Trikuza goons guarded the place and were serving as bouncers, sporting the usual assortment of tattoos that marked them as members of the criminal society. It wasn't the sort of place you'd expect a former lawyer of the Yakuza to spend their free time, but I wasn't a mob boss.

Paradise opened the side of the van and slid past Aiyumi to the outside. "This will take all of your skills, Kei! You've never had a mission like this before. You need to somehow prove yourself cool enough to get into this club despite being old enough to be a single mom!"

"I am not old eno..." I trailed off before I dug myself deeper.

Paradise grinned as I tried to work out a better response to that mess. I mean, it wasn't like you couldn't be old enough to be a single mother at a ridiculously young age. Also, I'd adopted a child who was now an adult but that was due to technological shenanigans! Besides, I was thirty and that was not remotely old!

"Do you have a plan?" Aiyumi asked.

"Do we need a plan?" I asked. "I mean, look at us. I've never seen a club that wasn't happy to let me in."

I plead the Fifth on the disaster that ensued. It shall be lost to the ages, forgotten, and spoken of no more by man nor beast. Instead, I shall resume my story past the humiliation back at the van where I was sitting on the edge with its side door open next to my remaining companions, minus two.

"Where does that bouncer get off!" I snapped. "Telling me to get to the back of the line!"

"He's doing his job," Aiyumi said.

"He let Paradise and Parvati in!"

"They're hotter than us," Aiyumi said, fitting in a lot better with her punk attire.

"They're not... okay, they are," I reluctantly conceded. "That doesn't make me feel any better about this!"

"You have a plan B to get in?" Case asked.

"You could dress sluttier!" Tom suggested.

I glared at him, then sighed. "I couldn't take being rejected a second time. We'll have to go in through the delivery entrance."

"This place has impressive security," Case said.

"It's a good thing we have skills," I said.

I admit, I started to think in a complicated *Mission Impossible* style that would include disabling security systems via hacking, taking out guards, and maybe going through in a skylight. I wanted to make a big impression on the Lady of Tigers and convince her that we were on the level. That we were worthy allying with. I admit, it felt invigorating to once more be out on a mission and I wanted to make sure I pulled this one off without a hitch. I wasn't very good at being a businesswoman and I hadn't quite succeeded at being a mother, but I was a damn good Runner and the skills for that were one part burglar as well as one part assassin. Neither of which would be thwarted by a gangster's club.

"Mrs. Gordon?" a thick male Japanese voice spoke to me.

I looked up and saw an abnormally tall man in a business suit with long black hair, smooth skin, and an impressive broad-shouldered body, wearing a pair of combat shades of the kind that bodyguards wore at Atlas Security's few competitors. Paradise was standing next to him as she gave a little wave to me.

"Uh, yes," I said, blinking. "Hi, Paradise."

"I went to the Lady of Tigers—who doesn't appreciate being called Toni or Tigra—and told her you wanted to see her," Paradise explained. "This is her bodyguard, Motoko. Say hi, Motoko.":

"Hello," Motoko said.

"No, you're supposed to say, 'hi Motoko,'" Paradise said, shaking her head. "See? This is what I'm working with."

Aiyumi looked up to the guy as if the Grim Reaper had suddenly made an appearance. He didn't even look at her.

"The Lady of Tigers will speak with you but only if you come alone and submit to a search," Motoko said, coldly. "Your falling out with the Chairman of the Cyber Dragons is well known but Tanaka-san's isn't."

"Tanaka-san?" I asked.

Aiyumi cleared her throat. "That would be me."

"You never asked her last name?" Case asked.

"It never came up!" I said, pausing. "I thought she only had one like Madonna."

Aiyumi had mentioned a few last names, but they'd been obvious aliases during our early friendship. I hadn't pried deeper and decided to ignore her use of them. In retrospect, maybe I should have pushed harder. Growing up among criminals, well, you didn't go around asking people their names. Half the names you heard were pseudonyms anyway. We will not discuss the year I was calling myself Bloodsword.

"I agree, Motoko," I said. "Lead the way." I did hope that this meeting-alone-after-surrendering-my-weapons ended better than my last one.

Case got up to follow me.

"Only her and the techjack," Motoko said, referring to me and Paradise. "We have enough assassins inside."

Case looked at me.

I nodded. "We'll be good. Tom can tell you police stories obviously adapted from TV shows."

Okay, that was cruel.

"I have other stories," Tom said. "Like, uh, okay, they're mostly adapted from TV shows, too."

"I'd love to hear them," Aiyumi said, faking lack of concern.

"Follow me," Motoko said.

They searched and disarmed me at the door, which left me feeling naked. Thankfully, they didn't insist on me being actually naked as some bosses had over the years. The interior of the

Tiger Club was pretty much the movie version of a night club. Most of the ones I attended were dark, cramped, usually in some building's basement, and the real appeal was in the alcohol as well as people wanting to get laid as much as you do. Here, it was much, much larger, great music, exotic light patterns, and still packed to the gills with people who were here to get drunk or laid or both. Amusingly, a song by Sun and QwantumCrab was playing, and I couldn't help but wonder how many fans would be still interested in her if they knew she was a digital goddess. Honestly, her popularity might have gone up in some circles.

We went up a spiraling glass staircase next to a private elevator that led to the second floor with a balcony view of the downstairs. It was full of large, overstuffed leather couches, deep purple carpet, and gold statue of a tiger at each corner of the room. Four was unlucky among Japanese culture and it was partially why the Neon Rat had never gotten his own clan according to Snake. Personally, I just believed no one wanted to give him that much power.

The VIP lounge reeked of Black Lotus and Red Dust in the air, the newer better versions of age-old drugs, and there were a half-dozen Trikuza leaders spread among the couch enjoying RealDream goggles. The expensive kind that worked just as well as a chair but cost about twenty grand each. A few of them weren't wearing them but those were bodyguards sporting guns despite Japan's absurdly strict—by American standards at least—gun laws.

It was easy to identify the Lady of Tigers since she dominated the room with her presence. I was reminded of Lucy Liu in Kill Bill despite the fact she wasn't Japanese like the Lady—it had even been a plot point!. The Lady of Tigers just had that vibe. Despite her reputation as the most "traditional" of the Trikuza, she was wearing a low cut strapless black Western dress with a slit and was smoking from a cigarette holder like Cruella Deville.

I'd have found it ridiculous, but she somehow made the look work. She had a very visible tiger tattoo on her right shoulder, even though most executives went without tattoos. That type of tattoo pretty much marked you as a criminal in Japanese culture. The tiger was crackling with electricity, but it wasn't made to glow like most Trikuza tattoos—she probably thought that was too much. Executives didn't usually rise from the ranks in the Yakuza and that had been part of the reason why the Trikuza had gotten off the ground. Even now, there were the goons and the guys (or girls) who went to business or law school.

I waited to be introduced. There were rules of etiquette that had been drilled into me by Snake when I was younger. I rarely had opportunity to use any of them, but I knew exactly how to pour tea for these people. Why any culture needed a specific way to pour tea had never made the slightest sense to me. Sure, it was a way to tell the in-group from the outsiders, but it was also a huge waste of time and effort. But, then, efficiency had never been the watchword. The Trikuza was in many ways a contradiction—it had added plenty of new rules and made up "traditions" whole cloth to compensate for all the ones it threw away.

"Onna-oyabun," Motoko said, basically saying, female boss. "I have brought the Daughter of the Cyber Dragons, and head of the Morrigans crime syndicate."

Paradise leaned in and whispered. "That's me."

"I know," I replied, annoyed.

"The Morrigans crime syndicate head part, not the Daughter of the Cyber Dragons," Paradise corrected.

Wow, she was being immensely rude. "Yeah."

"I think that's you," Paradise said, dodging away before I elbowed her in the gut.

"Come closer," the Lady of Tigers said. "I'm interested in talking with you."

I took a breath and stepped forward. "Madame. We know Snake is making a play for total control of the Trikuza. We would like to discuss an alternative."

"You can drop the act, Keiko," the Lady of Tigers said, surprising me. She also spoke in English.

"Excuse me?" I asked, surprised at her informality.

"Playing the dutiful Japanese daughter when you're an American raised by another American who helped found this organization that's a bastardization of our traditional values seems like it is one too many ironies," the Lady of Tigers said. "You also stabbed Snake in the chest, killed your adopted sister, worked to bring down Elysium, and have been trying to eliminate your mentor ever since. Winston was one of our operatives and an immortal abomination that was made of wires and information, but you killed him. So, let's not pretend I have any authority over you, or you have any respect for me."

"There are multiple forms of respect, and I certainly respect someone who commands enough guns in the room to blow my brains out," I said. "And I'm certainly not going to set out to deliberately offend you. But we can proceed. If you can keep Snake from assuming power, and oust him for his temerity, it will be much easier for us to kill him, which we believe would benefit you."

The Lady of Tigers put her cigarette in an ashtray, stood up, and walked—well slinked, really—toward one of the Trikuza executives enjoying a RealDream. She proceeded to put her hands around his neck and chin before snapping his neck with what was obviously enhanced strength.

The awake bodyguards and executives barely reacted, though a few fidgeted.

I stared. "Friend of yours?"

"A spy for Snake," the Lady of Tigers said. "I know his real name but, unlike in stories, it doesn't give me power over him. You realize that once you start this war, you won't be able to back away. Going after him directly is a fool's errand. These things are best handled with proxies. Boxes within boxes."

"He killed my mom," Paradise said, surprisingly lacking in her usual humor. "I take that personally."

The Lady of Tigers smiled and stared. "The real question is what exactly you think you can offer me to get the others to turn upon Snake. He's very popular, you know. Despite how ridiculous I find him to be, he's made a lot of recruits very rich and has been judicious with his violence. As much as I love the old way of doing things, his new way of doing things appeals to the over-caffeinated, sugar-addicted, infovision generation like Ms. Principle."

"Guns, we can give you guns," Paradise said. "He's also on the outs with the US President and Atlas Security. Whatever he brought to the table, he no longer brings, and we can continue. The next chairman of Atlas is out on the street."

The Lady of Tigers seemed intrigued. "And you, Kei? What are you willing to sacrifice and give to see this happen? What is the name that lies in your heart that drives you to kill this man so much? I know what names he's cost me and will be cost when he retaliates. What will be the cost when we have to exterminate his cult of men, women, and children?"

"Mine," I said. "He's wronged everyone I've known but it's my name that I name as the first of his victims."

"Good," the Lady of Tigers said, gesturing to a side door I'd barely noticed as it was disguised with no doorknob and identical paint to the rest of the wall.

That was when two men brought out Parvati, who looked like she'd been punched a few times and was now sporting the beginnings of a black eye.

"Not very host-like," I said, coldly.

"I planned to kill her in front of you as a way to show I wasn't to be trifled with, but you've convinced me," the Lady of Tigers said. "Give them back their weapons. We need to go to the Cherry Blossom Palace and present their accusations tonight before Snake's investiture."

"What accusations?" I asked, knowing but wanting to make absolutely sure we were on the same page.

"Treason, sedition, murder of fellow Trikuza," the Lady of Tigers said. "Turning you over to the Feds alongside many others. Whatever we can think up. All that matters is it's enough to justify his execution. Which you'll have the chance to do. Just make sure you get him."

I imagined them letting us kill Snake and then finishing us off.

This was a terrible plan.

Yet I was willing to go along with it.

CHAPTER TWENTY

THE STRONGHOLD OF THE TRIKUZA

Our group loaded up into two automated flying limousines prepared for us by the Lady of Tigers. I ended up beside Case, across from Parvati and Tom. Paradise and Aiyumi were inside the limousine with the Lady of Tigers and her bodyguard. Given that the last time I'd been in one of these vehicles, I'd been shot down and part of an assassination attempt that killed the President's mother, I was sort of iffy about the whole thing.

Also annoyed the Lady of Tigers didn't consider me worth talking to over Aiyumi. I briefly wondered if it was possibly a racism thing, with me being American and half-white, before deciding that, no, it was definitely racism. The Trikuza were significantly more open-minded than their Yakuza counterparts, but they were still operating from a criminal baseline. Contrary to what movies have taught us, it turns out most street criminals have some deeply repellent beliefs.

"So, we're all going to go to the Cherry Blossom Palace, meet with the Elemental Lords, they're going to kill Snake for us, and everything will be hunky dory," I said, looking across the distinctly familiar interior of the limousine. I was pretty sure it was another Atlas-produced model, even if not the exact same brand as the one that had been shot down. It only added to the eerie ambiance of the place.

"Yes," Parvati said, taking a deep breath. "That does seem to be our current plan."

"Even though we're going to walking into the lion's—well, tiger's den—and it's very probable that Snake will resist," I replied, not happy about it. I also wasn't happy about the beating that Parvati took even though it could have been much worse. It was a reminder that the Lady of Tigers wasn't on our side so much as temporarily aligned with our goals—and even that was questionable.

"Not just Snake," Tom said, cheerfully. "Probably however many other child soldiers he's brainwashed into becoming his personal army of killers."

"They're all adults by the time Snake deploys them," Case corrected Tom, reaching over to the mini bar and finding a decidedly Western collection of alcoholic beverages.

"Oh, my mistake," Tom said. "What should we call them instead. Cultists?"

"Ninjas," I replied. "Because if we're going to be hunting down my old boss/mentor/sensei/father figure, we might as well call them ninjas. We're already in an action movie."

"Yeah," Parvati said, looking down at the floor.

"So, you haven't exactly been chatty since we joined up at the airport," I said, hoping to break the ice. "What have you been up to since, well, uh—"

"I left you guys after our horrifying failure to prevent a coup against the United States government?" Parvati asked.

I stared at her, unsure how to respond. "To be fair, we weren't trying to prevent a coup against the US government. We were trying to stop the Trikuza from blackmailing a bunch of politicians and millionaires after turning them into serial killers."

"Our lives are kind of terrifying when you put it that way," Tom said, making a joke that, going by our expressions, none of us seemed to find particularly funny.

"Pour me one of those," Parvati said, seeing Case had gotten himself a decanter of bourbon.

"Me too," I interjected. "The Trikuza is paying after all."

"Me three," Tommy said. "Also, aren't you a billionaire now?"

"Technically, only Case is," I replied.

"No prenup from what I hear," Parvati said, pointing at me with finger guns in an exaggeratedly happy way. "So, it's cheaper to kill you than divorce you."

I frowned at her as Case handed me a full glass, lacking ice. "Hilarious."

Parvati had the decency to look ashamed. "Yeah, I'm not exactly as funny as I used to be."

I thought back to our brief time together. "To be fair, I never thought you were funny in the first place. You were always the hardass Magistrate trying to bring down a bunch of people higher up in the food chain."

Being a Magistrate had been Parvati's dream job and I knew she'd felt adrift and alone after losing it.

"Yeah, I broke the second most important rule in law enforcement after don't rat out other cops," Parvati said, sighing. "Don't mess with the money."

"Well, at least the twenty million credit payoff must have softened the blow," Case said, joining our conversation.

Case was referring to the "gift" that Snake and President Alders had sent us after our role in the Elysium massacre. It was a payout designed to keep us quiet if we somehow managed to survive the event, which we did. While a massive payout to individuals, it was pocket change to the US government, even in its diminished state. The money had helped build Ares Electronics and I wasn't ashamed of taking it and putting it to good use.

I took a sip pf my bourbon. I wasn't a connoisseur, liquor existed to get you drunk and anything else was just gravy. Which I would have killed for, literally, at various points in my life. "Yeah."

Parvati looked guilty. "I kind of gave that all away."

I choked on my next sip before taking a much larger drink. "You did *what*?"

There was moral and there was stupid. This was something I considered to be stupid.

"It was blood money," Parvati said, as if I didn't know that.

"It was twenty million credits," I said, as if that was enough. "Like forty million new dollars."

Tom looked like he wanted to agree with me before sucking in his breath and supporting his girlfriend instead. "It was the right thing to do."

Parvati shook her head. "Some children are going to receive life-saving medical treatments that they'd otherwise not be able to have. Maybe a lot of them and that's going to give my life meaning. That's all I can say right now, especially given where we're heading."

There was a certain finality to her tone that surprised me.

I stared at her. "You don't think we're coming back from this, do you?"

Parvati's expression was grave. Resigned even. "Kei, you and Case have survived more bloody shootouts and close calls than anyone else I've ever met, and I've met some real badasses over the years. However, there's a simple rule of gambling: eventually you lose. That's never truer than when you're playing with your life."

I narrowed my eyes. "I'm not playing a game."

"I know," Parvati said. "But we are. I'm also willing to pay the price to see Snake brought to justice."

I shook my head. "We're not going to die here, Parvati. We're all going to come back from this. I'm not going to sacrifice your lives to get my revenge."

Parvati looked skeptical. "Aren't you?"

I stared at Tom. "Talk her out of this."

Tom looked away. "Where she goes, I go."

I felt suddenly ganged up on and they were technically on my side in all of this. "Really?"

"I was made to deliver Not-Jennifer Lawrence to you as well as run interference for Sun," Tom replied, looking bitter about it. "I wasn't even born to play a starring role in my own life. I was made to be a bit player in someone else's drama. But I'm alive now and I'm willing to risk that because I've found something that makes that meaningful. I bet Case and the others feel the same."

I stared at them both, uncomprehending. "Why would you two risk your lives for this? Snake didn't..."

Well, I almost said ruin your lives, but he had. Parvati had been fired from being a Magistrate and made party to the coup against the United States government she loved. She had that patriotism only found in the children of immigrants, Snake had made her party not only to the mass murder of innocents at Elysium but also every death that had resulted from Diane Alders' wars of aggression since, which had only happened to show that the United States wasn't the crippled shell of a superpower it had become.

"Justice," Parvati said. "Maybe it is a stupid concept to believe in these days, but I do."

"Yeah," I replied.

Which made me feel like a massive hypocrite.

And maybe I was.

"We're here," Case muttered, staring out over the side.

I looked out the window of the limousine and saw the Cherry Blossom Palace coming up. It was a massive estate done in a traditional Japanese style, only much, much bigger. The Trikuza had once just been three minor Yakuza clans that had been on the outs with the rest of organized crime when they'd decided to take advantage of America's fallen state and open themselves up to outsiders.

Somehow, probably with the help of AI recognizing people needed diversions, they'd managed to find themselves at the head of the world's largest crime syndicate. While there were maybe thirty thousand Yakuza left in Japan, there were something like two hundred thousand Trikuza globally with their ranks swollen with more recruits every year.

Still, Snake was the highest-ranking Westerner among them and the only one of the Elemental Lords who couldn't trace his lineage to one of the original clans like the Tanaguchi-yumi or Shimiyoshi-kai. The fact they instead went by names like Lightning Phoenixes, Cyber Dragons, or Electric Tigers also highlighted that they were posers who'd made it big. Big enough to build a compound that seemed to stretch on and on.

The biggest irony? The majority of the Trikuza's money came from legitimate construction, gambling, nightclubs, porn, and check cashing places rather than their directly criminal dealings. They didn't *need* to engage in drugs, human trafficking, and murder to be richer than God, or the kami in this case.

"Ever been here?" Parvati asked, looking at me.

"A few times," I replied. "Snake made me wear a kimono

and kept pointing out all the historical stuff they'd stolen from other, real Yakuza and their history. I think he was more interested in fitting in than I was."

"Well, we're going to be arriving as honored guests," Case said. "Which will do absolutely nothing when they turn their guns on us and kill all of us."

"I sense the mood is not exactly jubilant," I said, putting my best sarcastic voice on. "I take it you don't believe the Elemental Lords will deal with us fairly, either?"

"We've already failed the mission they gave us," Case replied. "Plus, we know too much."

I tried to figure out what he meant. "Excuse me?"

Case stared. "Winston said he was working for the other Elemental Lords in wanting to kill Snake. Now he's dead and Snake is still alive."

I blinked. I'd thought Winston had just been making that up. "Wait, you think the Lady of Tigers was behind Winston?"

"Yes," Case said. "Not just her either. I think they were behind the entire plan. They would frame Snake for killing Samantha then kill us. It's probably why Winston let loose the Ken portion of their brain. It partitioned his personality so they could do the second part of the mission freely."

"Do you have any idea what they're talking about?" Parvati asked.

"No," Tom said.

"So, what, Snake gets framed but screws up their plans to eliminate him by showing up at HQ?" I asked, feeling the flying car start to descend.

"Yes," Case said. "Probably with his followers so that just killing him isn't an option."

"Now we're heading…" I trailed off. "This feels like a theory you should have shared earlier."

"I admit, I only came up with it now," Case said, looking sheepish.

I hit him on the arm. "Be more paranoid."

"No one in history has ever suggested that to me before," Case said, looking offended. "I will someday prove the Invisible Hand is real."

"Be paranoid about real things!" I said, feeling the limousine hit the ground with a light thump.

I felt something akin to anticipation despite the fact we were probably walking into a trap. Snake was nearby, I could feel it, and our final confrontation would be soon. I'd been running from him virtually my entire adult life and the fact I wasn't anymore felt like its own triumph. However small a victory, I could tell myself that I was no longer afraid of the man who'd taken me from my family.

Looking out the window, I saw a large flying car landing pad that was full of vehicles. It was surrounded by gravel and a little tiny bit of garden that felt more like a commercialized image of Japan than authentically Japanese despite, you know, being in Japan. There were a lot of people here, including us, and it made me uncomfortable. Clearly, we were stepping into something big tonight. It had been a decade since I'd last set foot here, but the Cherry Blossom Palace wasn't usually full to capacity given its size.

"Ever feel you've stepped in it but aren't sure what it is?" I asked, watching the doors to the limousine raise up to let us out.

"Every day of my life," Tom muttered. "Which turns out to have not been that long."

"Yeah, I had that problem," Case said, getting out of the car. A light rain had started, which was common in Japan—well, common everywhere but especially on a rainy island. Case, much to my surprise pulled out a small umbrella from his coat pocket, which really showed the guy was prepared for anything at all times. "Let's go meet with the rest of our group and see what wonderful twists and turns our not-so-trustworthy allies have in store for us."

"You're awfully cheery for someone who believes we're about to be betrayed," I said, looking at my husband.

"Fear is the avoidance of death, courage is the acceptance," Case said.

"That's a stupid saying," I said, uncomfortable with how close it was to what Parvati and Tom had been saying.

"When seeking revenge, dig two graves—" Tom started to quote the proverb.

"Yeah, I've seen *For Your Eyes Only*," I muttered. "Case made me watch the entirety of the Bond series. All thirty-six movies. Idris Elba was my favorite."

"Uh huh," Parvati said.

It was easy to spot Paradise, Aiyumi, the Lady of Tigers, and Motoko. The man sort of towered over everyone else. Approaching them, I noticed a traditionally dressed Japanese woman who had a strong resemblance to Aiyumi next to a man I recognized from my time with Snake. The man was Tanaka Akio, basically Snake's butler. He rarely showed up at the apartment where Snake had me living, but I'd seen him often enough to have the toady's memory burned into my brain.

Maybe it was wrong to hold Akio's service to Snake against him, but the guy had always acted fawning and sycophantic to Snake. He'd known about us being essentially Snake's slaves, yet he had never done anything for us but make sure we'd been fed, clothed, and sheltered. He barely spoke a word to us and when he did, it was always just to tell us to obey Snake.

"Look what the tiger dragged in," I muttered, glaring at Akio. "Maybe I should have followed your slime trail here, Akio."

Aiyumi cleared her throat. "I see you know my father, Kei."

I closed my eyes and wished I was dead at that moment. "Huh. Small world."

"And getting smaller," the Lady of Tigers said. "Lady Tanaka Hana will be serving as Snake's speaker until his arrival at the meeting. He's currently in meditation."

The woman I presumed to be Aiyumi's mother looked at me with a snake's smile. "The Lord of the Cyber Dragons looks forward to seeing his wayward apprentice."

"The rest of the Elemental Lords wish to speak with us now, though," the Lady of Tigers said, gesturing to a nearby paper doorway that opened. "The other oyabun and their lieutenants have already started discussing events without me."

There was only the slightest hint of emotion behind her words. Unfortunately, that emotion was fear.

CHAPTER TWENTY-ONE

CURSE THEIR SUDDEN BUT INEVITABLE BETRAYAL

"Please follow us," Hana gestured.

"So, I take it that our advantage of surprise is utterly spoiled?" I asked the Lady of Tigers.

"There was never a way to have this meeting happen without Snake being made aware," the Lady of Tigers replied. "The issue is getting him into check first in order to bring him to checkmate."

"And now we're discussing it right in front of them," I muttered. "I wish you'd informed us this was your plan."

"Where's the fun in that?" the Lady of Tigers asked, starting to walk to the Cherry Blossom Palace's closest entrance.

We followed.

"It's alright," Aiyumi said, surprising me. "Snake's soldiers will not be the ones to break the truce first. If the Lady of Tigers brings charges against Snake among the Trikuza, it must be done publicly and devastatingly."

"Two of his students unveiling his crimes will be enough to do much damage," the Lady of Tigers said. "Especially when they discover just how badly his position has degraded among Atlas and the United States."

"I would not be so sure," I muttered, having a bad feeling about all this.

"It will work," the Lady of Tigers tried to reassure me despite the fact I'd momentarily seen behind her mask. She was playing the confident woman, but this was an all or nothing move. If she brought charges against Snake and he was acquitted, he'd be well in his rights to move against her in the same way.

But perhaps better that then serving under Emperor Snake. Nah, that didn't sound right: the Snake Emperor.

"I would think that the latter would be fairly well-known," I said. "Surely, the United States has been trying to get people to help kill him by now."

"Whoever said talk is cheap has never worked in intelligence," Case said, following behind me. "No one is announcing Snake's involvement in Samantha Sanders' death publicly. It's being kept within the highest circles of power."

"Which means everyone is discussing it, but no one has any facts," the Lady of Tigers said.

"It is a problem that will be resolved soon enough," Hana replied, looking back at me. "The real culprits will be turned over and punished."

That wasn't a good sign. "Yeah."

Our not-so-little group was led down the halls of the Cherry Blossom Palace as I soaked in how the place still felt like it had when I was a teenager: like someone's cheap knockoff of a real gangster's palace. If someone had created Scarface's mansion from, well, *Scarface*, but it was from a heretofore unknown Japanese version, and then had a billion dollars to spend on building the place, well, it would look exactly like this. It was like a hotel for gangsters with long hallways, endless numbers of rooms, and things that were meant to look like priceless art but were really mass-produced knockoffs.

The Trikuza was essentially a funhouse mirror of the real Yakuza that had somehow replaced the originals in influence. I wasn't a great believer that the Yakuza were anything worth admiring but it was like someone had watched a huge number of movies then somehow decided they showed how actual gangsters acted. The fact it had worked, had even thrived, in the new world was galling on a level that could only be appreciated by someone who'd once fully embraced the kitsch world of honor and blood they'd preached as a philosophy.

The fact I passed dozens of heavily-tattooed thugs of both sexes as well as several ethnicities also lent itself to the weird feeling I got. They were members of the three separate Clans of the Trikuza as well as their sub-gangs. A lot of them. That was notable because the majority of guys with tattoos—a major no-no in Japan—would normally not be let into the HQ proper. There was a separation between the soldiers and the executives that never really was crossed except in fiction. Oh, and with Snake.

Yep, crap was going down tonight.

Probably long before we arrived.

"So, Aiyumi," Paradise said, allergic to silence. "Your parents are like Snake's slaves, huh?"

"Associates," Hana said, having a thick accent for her Japanese. Which I found to be almost insulting since I was pretty sure everyone here spoke the local language or at least had translator programs.

"Yes," Aiyumi interrupted. "It appears when they sold me to Snake, they decided that their destiny was better served with the Trikuza. They are now high-ranking lieutenants of the Cyber Dragons."

I almost scoffed at this because Akio as a lieutenant was only slightly more believable than Fredo being the boss of the Corleone family. Then I realized it was another bad sign because it meant that Snake had been stacking the deck for any upcoming political conflict.

"We did *not* sell you to Snake," Akio said, his voice surprisingly defensive. "It was meant to be an honor to be his student."

"Meant to be?" I snapped at her. "Do you have the slightest idea what he did to us?! The surgeries? The emotional torture?"

"Save it for the big meetup," Paradise said. "Don't want you getting exhausted now."

I didn't have a response to that. This was a dog and pony show. Our role here was to show that Snake was someone who wasn't a wise and beneficent mentor, but someone who threw his people under the bus. The Trikuza didn't value loyalty—everyone was disposable—but that didn't mean that they didn't pretend otherwise. Just like the US mafia, the goal was to make sure you thought of them as family and they followed a code when the truth was to benefit the higher-ups with your blood, sweat, and tears. Damn, Paradise was right. I should be saving this.

We passed through a set of double doors that opened up to a large audience chamber that looked more like a basketball court than a meeting room. There were gymnasium-style bleachers set up and probably over a hundred people present: not just the Japanese higher-ups but people from United Korea's mobs, Vietnam, China, and, of course, the United States. It was the kind of group that would never normally be in one room together despite the corporatization of organized crime Post-Eruption but were uncomfortably sitting together.

The end of the room had four literal thrones on a raised dais with two individuals already seated. It was a more Western movie or fantasy novel court than a typical one, but that was the international nature of the group in action. A square skylight showed the moon hanging in the sky above and there was a large empty space beneath that we were shuffled to. I also recognized some of Snake's people. They were the people not in suits, but who dressed like supervillains. One guy was even in carbon fiber samurai armor and another with what looked like steel skin. Had I really looked this ridiculous when I was a member of the Trikuza?

Okay, yeah, yeah, I had.

The Lord of Storms was a Japanese man—I know, shocking—in his late thirties, with a slight resemblance to Motoko. He was young for his position and dressed in a formal kimono that was probably a couple of centuries old. He was wearing it uncomfortably and I could tell he was playing up his ancestry as well as tradition versus his reputation as a progressive. Yeah, my ninja-senses were on full alert here. It made the "frick me" dress the Lady of Tigers was wearing take on a new contrast as she wore hers to make herself seem more approachable. Clothing as armor against political weakness.

Another throne had the Neon Rat, and he was wearing a white fur coat that made him like a particularly sleazy pimp. He was Japanese of course, overweight, his face covered in pox marks that you had to wonder about the origins of, and he had a pair of small, round glasses that reminded me a bit of the villain's in *Raiders of the Lost Ark*. The Neon Rat and I had only had a few encounters in our lives but the first time we'd met, he'd asked

Snake to let him "break me in." Snake had responded by threat-ening to break his wrist but, apparently, they were friends now.

But there was no sign of Snake. Why wasn't Snake here? Did he see value in a late entrance, or did he have other plans? I wouldn't entirely be surprised if he tried killing us all with a remote or something.

In any case, these were the feudal lords who would be deciding if I lived or died in the metaphorical arena. I prob-ably would have been less nervous entering an actual arena. Nothing to do now but wait for the festivities to start.

A woman in a porcelain Chesire Cat mask walked up with a silver tray in her hands, filled with little earpieces. "Translators."

I was good but took one anyway. My Japanese might have been heavily accented despite my best efforts, but I could under-stand it perfectly. My mother had insisted on it and Snake had spoken as often in it as English to make sure I mastered it. Everyone else took one as well and I noticed Aiyumi looking at the cat girl.

"Tatski," Aiyumi said. "How much trouble are we in?"

The woman, apparently Tatski, made a shh gesture.

Aiyumi looked at me. She proceeded to speak with me via infolink. *Yeah, we're screwed.*

How badly? I asked, watching the Lady of Tigers walk up and take her seat on the throne.

Badly, Aiyumi replied. *Tatski says that Snake is going to mount a coup tonight and it's going to be a violent one. This was all theater to get his enemies in one place before he made an attempt to assassinate them all. She might be willing to help us escape but I don't think we can rely on her to help against Snake. There are a lot of debts she has against the others.*

You got all that from a shh gesture? I asked via our infolink. *When is this happening? How well do you know this person?*

That part she didn't say, Aiyumi said. *She's basically my version of Paradise.*

There's a Japanese version of me? Paradise asked, horrified. *How? What? Why? I'll sue.*

How are you on this link? Aiyumi asked. *It's encrypted by digital gods. By which I mean Barbara and Trish.*

I am the legendary techjack dataslicer known as P@r@dise! Paradise said. *I know, it's shocking. No one has figured out my identity in years.*

"God," I muttered, aloud.

The @ symbols look like boobs, Paradise said. *Either that or big wide eyes like the Hooters logo. Hooters was a legendary corporation that introduced buffalo wings to mankind. It had something to do with owls.*

These people have to be expecting something of the sort, I said. *They can't have put a moonroof that big in here and not have expected someone to rappel in at some point.*

Maybe they've never seen an action movie, Paradise said.

Look around you! These people have based their lives on action movies! I said. *Bad ones!*

Yes, many of them must know about Snake's plans, but obviously not enough or the ones that know about it think they will be spared. The question now is should we warn them, Aiyumi said.

Wait, why would we not warn them? I asked, confused. *We're here for Snake.*

And this might be the diversion needed to distract his forces, Aiyumi replied. *Bluntly, the Trikuza is a collection of murderers, slavers, and predators on humanity's addictions. At their sacrifice, we might be able to strike a killing blow to our target and leave them all in disarray.*

I'm surprised you have that attitude, Paradise said. *I would have thought some of these people were your friends.*

My family is Trikuza, Aiyumi said. *But they are not the people I love. Nor do they love me. That is something Kei taught me.*

I wasn't sure that was the lesson I'd wanted to teach Aiyumi but that was when I noticed the Lord of Storms was speaking. "We have some unexpected guests tonight and accusations to address. All of you have heard of the changes that have happened to our relationship with the Atlas Corporation. When the Cyber Dragon's chairman cost us Elysium, he made up for it by a newer, stronger relationship with the US government."

There was dead silence in the room, but I could tell by some expressions that not everyone was happy with that association.

We have to decide now what we're going to do, Aiyumi said.

Whatever is going to happen is going to happen soon.

We tell the Tiger, I said, deciding. *We owe her that much for bringing us this far. Though a lot depends on how she reacts to that.*

You owe her nothing, Aiyumi said, sharper than I expected.

You really don't like her, do you? I asked, surprised.

The Lady of Tigers was the one my mother and father owed their debts to, Aiyumi replied.

I tried to contact the Lady of Tigers' own implant, before realizing she didn't have one. She was entirely organic.

Great.

Didn't even have a cell phone in that outfit.

"Dammit," I cursed under my breath.

The Lord of Storms was still talking. "Today we must make a decision as to which way we must go as a group. We must decide whether to follow Snake into a new road that may lead us to making enemies of our former allies or to punish him for exceeding his—"

I decided to be incredibly stupid. I interrupted the Lord of Storms' speech and shouted in Japanese. "Snake is going to kill everyone here!"

That was when Tatski, who'd somehow hidden behind the Lord of Storms without me even seeing her move, slit his throat from behind with a thermal knife.

Snake's people started opening fire into the crowd.

Oh frick.

"Nobody's actually rappelling," Paradise said. "I'm so disappointed!"

"Get down!" I shouted.

That was when—in one of those rare moments when life imitates art—people did start rappelling down through the sky-light. I would have laughed at the absurdity of it, but people were dying, and it wasn't Snake's people who started opening fire into the crowds above us.

No, it was someone far more dangerous: the US military. Or Atlas Special Operations, called the Special Task Force Unit or STFU—which I only then realized was a clever acronym. The two were not exactly a separate group these days. A bunch of black-armored, helmeted, cybernetically enhanced guys with reputations that had been affirmed in all of Diane Alders' wars. By Case's astonished expression, they weren't here to help us. They were here to kill Snake, too.

As well as anyone around him.

Unfortunately, for them, they were also surrounded by a bunch of ninjas as well as what turned out to be a bunch of gangsters who weren't nearly as unarmed as they appeared to be. We would have been cut down ourselves if not for the fact that sheer luck seemed to be on our side. Motoko charged forward, drawing a thermal sword and slicing away at service men as more soldiers could be heard entering from other entrances nearby. Motoko wanted to protect his lady more than anything, but both were caught by a thrown grenade.

Seriously, grenades?

It was ignominious end for the Lady of Tigers who had, despite being a complete witch, impressed me in our short time knowing one another.

There was no sign of the Neon Rat.

Case grabbed one of the fallen soldiers' M781 assault cannon as Aiyumi grabbed another off the ground. It was pure chaos as plenty of gangsters decided to flee rather than engage in more battle. I saw a couple of bullets strike against Case's back, but his suits were armored and his skin synthetic over bulletproof muscle. Yeah, there now was gunfire coming from the skylight.

Parvati and Tom were separated from us in the crowd as we made our own attempts to exit the kill zone. Paradise ended up being tossed another of the cannons by Tatski, of all people, before she vanished before my eyes.

Optical camouflage.

"Die, traitor!" The guy in the samurai costume said, raising up an A-17 submachine gun point blank at my face. I gave a jab at his throat with full force, crushing his windpipe in a blow that could only happen due to my enhancements. He fell to the ground, choking to death, before I grabbed his weapon.

That was when I started shooting and created an exit for us into the halls.

CHAPTER TWENTY-TWO

ONE OF US IS LEAVING THIS PALACE ALIVE

The sounds of gunfire, screams, and shouting interacted with the weird elevator music playing in the background. I didn't know why the Trikuza had chosen to play melodies in the background of their headquarters, but it just added to the weird ambiance of it all. There was nothing like shooting people to the sounds of Japanese orchestra. I had to wonder if it had been playing before and I just didn't notice it because I'd been lost in my thoughts or if someone had absurdly decided to turn it on during the mayhem.

I didn't hesitate to shoot the people trying to kill me, whether they were Snake's people, the Four Elemental Lords', or Atlas Security mercenaries. All three of them were fully prepared to kill me and I was fully prepared to kill them in return.

"We need to fall back," Aiyumi said, covering my back as Paradise and Case carried their assault cannons. Paradise looked particularly ridiculous carrying the giant gun but somehow managed to handle it with no difficulties.

"No!" I snapped. "Snake is here! We can end this!"

It was, on the surface, an utterly ridiculous statement. We were presently under attack by what seemed to be a full-on military invasion by the US government's black ops division and that was on top of a civil war between the Cyber Dragons' leadership. Snake was finished. Hell, Snake had been finished without our involvement and I was just one more person who wanted him dead when the entire world was crashing down on his head.

"Kei, we are going to die!" Paradise said, showing uncharacteristic concern.

We were already falling back into the interior of the Cherry Blossom palace rather than toward the exit and a part of me understood just how utterly insane this was. We'd already been separated from Parvati and Tom. I had no idea whether they were living or dead. Both had been willing to help in this quest for revenge and they'd been friends. Not close ones, but people that deserved better than to die for my revenge.

"We can't just leave!" I said plaintively as we entered a beautiful lounge that all of us ducked into as one wall started filling with massive bullet holes from someone firing a chain gun from somewhere up to a few hallways down. That was a fact that movies rarely pointed out—unless you had specially-crafted ammunition, bullets often pierce walls and hit things you weren't aiming at. Thankfully, none of us were in front of it when it happened but it underscored just how chaotic and out of control this battlefield was.

"On the contrary," Paradise said, trying to fake cheerfulness but looking genuinely terrified for possibly the first time in her life. "I believe we very much can flee out of this place. The question is if that's even possible."

"You have the map, Paradise," Case said, dryly.

"Right!" Paradise said, kneeling and holding her head. "I do!"

A young Trikuza punk, he couldn't have been more than nineteen, ran into the room with a pistol and fired at Case. He shot him twice in the chest and once in the shoulder, Case's body armor absorbed it all, but my husband casually raised his hand and put a bullet in the kid's forehead. The boy landed on the ground, his face obliterated. It made me wonder which side of this he'd been on or if it even mattered at his age.

"Fine," I said, pausing. "Get us an exit."

I hated myself for saying it and wanted to scream or argue but logic acted against me. Snake could be in any one of these two hundred rooms and barring a miracle, our chances of finding him before STFU killed us were low. Hell, it wasn't like Snake's people or the Trikuza's goons weren't capable of killing us either.

Unfortunately, God took his or her time to deliver me a miracle at exactly the wrong time. Tom contacted me on my info-link. *Kei, can you hear me? I've got eyes on Snake and some of his people. Two of them. They're in the Dragon Room.*

The what? I asked.

The room with all the dragons! Tom said, as if I was being an idiot. *We're ready to engage but could use some backup.*

I knew how utterly suicidal that would be. Snake may have bought his superhuman speed, strength, and durability but he still had it. It was the equivalent of assaulting a tank with a pistol. *Hold out. I'll be right there.*

Case looked at me, clearly recognizing that I'd been contacted and what the nature of the contact was. "Don't go."

"I have to," I said, lying. This wasn't about Parvati and Tom. This was about me and my stupid desire for revenge. Still, I was glad to have the excuse to hide behind. "Paradise, where is the Dragon Room?"

"Are you serious?" Paradise asked, staring at me.

I stared back at her. "Yes."

"We'll be behind you," Case muttered. "Until the end."

"No," I said, sucking in my breath. It wasn't because I couldn't use the help against Snake, but because the one time that Case had faced him, he'd gotten his ass handed to him. My husband had once been the world's best assassin, but he was definitely of the disguise, sneak around, and kill from a distance kind than actual fighting. Which, honestly, probably made him much better than Snake ever was. But he couldn't help here, and I was scared to death he'd get himself killed trying to help me. Unfortunately, I could see Paradise and Case were already assuming it was their job to protect me. "I need you two to figure out a way to get us the hell out of this place after I kill Snake and rescue our friends."

"I am coming with you," Aiyumi said, lifting her submachine gun.

I could hear the fighting getting a bit more distant and less fierce, which indicated one side or another was winning. Call me crazy, but I was pretty sure it was the professional soldiers and their heavy weaponry.

"No," I started to say.

"You can't win alone," Aiyumi said, walking past me. "The Dragon Room is down this hallway."

Crap.

"She's right," Paradise said. "We'll work on an exit strategy. Try not to get killed."

"Keep her safe, Case," I said to my husband.

"I will." Case nodded.

We exchanged a kiss, short and to the point. I just hoped that it wouldn't be the final one.

"Hey!" Paradise said, frowning.

"As I'm sure she'll protect me," Case said.

I nodded then ran after Aiyumi. "Did you actually mean it when you said you don't think I can win?"

"No," Aiyumi said, walking boldly down the ornate hallways of the Cherry Blossom Palace. "I *know* you can't win."

"I've beaten you plenty of times," I muttered, keeping my hands on my gun.

"I let you win," Aiyumi said. "It was part of my attempt to ingratiate myself with you."

"Which time?" I asked, not that surprised. Aiyumi had often pretended to be less skilled than she was. I'd just assumed she was trying to not hurt my feelings. I hadn't exactly been keeping up with my hand-to-hand skills for the year I'd been watching over Becky. Dammit, Trish. I was going to get used to her name, someday.

Unfortunately, our journey was almost immediately cut short by the sight of many bodies that had been gunned down without ceremony. They were a combination of servants and other lower members of the Trikuza who had clearly decided to nope the frick out of the conflict, only to get caught by someone else on their way out. That someone might have been the Atlas Special Forces or Snake's people, but the result was the same.

"Dammit," I muttered, stepping around the bodies. "It looks like D-Day here."

I immediately regretted my joke when I saw one of the bodies on the ground was Aiyumi's mother, Hana. She'd been caught in the back with a bullet and bled out on the ground. It was enough to make me want to vomit.

"Oh God, I am so sorry," I said, looking around and seeing that Aiyumi had stopped a little further up.

Her father was dead, too.

"It's not your doing, Kei," Aiyumi replied, resuming her stride through the hallway. "This is war."

"It's not a war," I muttered, feeling sick and wondering if I was partially responsible for this. "It's a bunch of petty people fighting over pride and getting a bunch of other people killed in the process."

Aiyumi didn't look back. "That is war."

I had to admit I both admired and pitied Aiyumi in that moment. I'd never been the kind of stoic badass that Snake had tried to warp me into. However, I had to wonder how much of that was perception versus reality. I'd seen past the hardened exterior of Aiyumi and beneath was a girl who liked video games and probably preferred to hang out with Paradise instead of me. Yet, here she was, preparing to fight on my behalf for a cause she wasn't even entirely onboard with until a few days ago.

Was this leadership on my part? Friendship? Family? I didn't have an answer, and it bothered the hell out of me. Yet, I couldn't figure out how to not do what I was doing. I kept moving forward, even when I wanted to stop to check myself. What would happen if I died on this mission? Who would I leave behind? What if Aiyumi got killed here? Tom and Parvati were depending on us, but they would be torn to shreds by Snake.

I couldn't say I didn't know what I was doing when I started all of this, but it was only now hitting me emotionally that I'd long since lost control over my quest for revenge: Samantha Sanders, her bodyguard, the Ken part of Winston, the Lady of Tigers, Aiyumi's parents, and who knew how many others had already died.

When would be *enough*?

It occurred to me, possibly for the first time, that even if I did kill Snake it might not be the end. I'd been so focused on my revenge that I hadn't even thought about the fact that Snake still had followers who loved him like a god or father. What if I killed him and this whole thing became a generational struggle with one of the other students coming after me or Trish? What if I died and I devastated those handful of people in the world I still cared about and who cared about me? All these kinds of thoughts would have been great to have earlier. However, I doubt I would have been able to stop myself.

In a way, it was a relief when the ninjas attacked.

Yeah, that was my life in a nutshell. Ninjas attacking was just a thing you could say without irony. We were passing by a paper wall when they smashed through and grabbed our weapons, throwing us against the side of the hallway before attempting to turn them on us.

To be fair, they didn't *look* like ninjas but that was the nature of the beast that there was no actual look for them outside of action movies and cartoons. No one actually wore the pajamas, and they remained covert by going in disguise. These particular ninjas didn't look remotely covert, but they didn't have to for me to recognize Snake's telltale handiwork. It was in their every deadly movement.

The first one had hair the fiery red you only found in animation, bright to the point of almost neon. She had bright, glowing tattoos on her arms, chest, and legs that were visible because she was wearing a sleeveless tank top with shorts. Her skin pressed against me was like hardened rubber and I suspected she was a far less sophisticated form of Shell than most.

Which was probably the only way I had a snowball's chance in hell.

The second was a white-haired Black man with a pair of glowing lightning tattoos on his cheek. He was wearing a blue denim jacket and pants with a simple neon green t-shirt. He'd managed to grab Aiyumi's wrists and delivered an electrical shock from his hands that I noticed were artificial and possessed no skin whatsoever. The guy was a living Taser and caused her to spasm out, which was a strong opening move.

"Mother sucker!" I muttered as the redhead, who I mentally named Red for no better reason than to call her something, tried to push my gun under my chin.

"Death to the traitor!" Red hissed, showing the kind of

originality that Snake fostered in his students.

Instead, I pulled the trigger on the gun prematurely and caused her to flinch back before I unloaded in her chest at point blank. She was almost entirely artificial by the number of sparks and explosion of white cyber-blood that coated me. Unfortunately, Red didn't seem to be particularly bothered as she ripped the gun from my hand before casting it to one side, going for my throat. Apparently, we were at the strangling portion of our encounter.

I wasn't all snark and sass, though, and went for the thermal knife in my boot as I ducked under their arms before she attacked. I got behind her in one easy motion and jabbed the weapon into the back of the cyborg's brain with a burning, hissing noise that was accompanied by an inhuman screech. Red's body ceased moving and collapsed against the side of the wall like a puppet whose strings had been cut. The knife kept burning in the back of her despite no longer being necessary.

"Murderer!" Blue, because I was equally creative in my vocabulary, screamed at the death of his partner.

It was a grossly hypocritical statement, but when you're fighting for your life and those of the people around you, the details of who did what and when sort of faded away. Blue went for me, only to have Aiyumi grab her submachine gun off the ground and blast him repeatedly in the back. Blue staggered for a second and was frozen in place by the attack. I suspected he wasn't quite as enhanced as the late Red.

"Sorry, pal," I said, grabbing the thermal knife out of Red's skull and stabbing Blue in the side of his head. It was a brutal but simple motion that brought an end to yet another one of Snake's students. He fell to the ground, and I left the knife where it lay. It was running out of its charge anyway.

"Poor Charles and Mari," Aiyumi muttered, surveying the pair of corpses before us. She was on one knee, looking like the electrical attack had taken a lot out of her.

"You knew these two?" I asked, surprised.

"Yes," Aiyumi said. "They were never the best of Snake's students, but they had each other, so it didn't matter."

"I'm sorry," I said.

"Don't be," Aiyumi said, climbing to her feet. "They were probably the ones who carried out the massacre down the hall."

I wanted to argue the point but wasn't sure why. An eerie silence had settled over the Cherry Blossom Palace and whatever fighting had been going on was over now. To say it made me nervous was greatly understating things.

"Tom, are you there?" I asked, deciding to check in. "Parvati? Paradise? Case?"

Silence.

Crap.

"We should head back," I said, suddenly no longer thinking about Snake. It was like a light switch had been flipped and all I could think about was my husband and few remaining friends—all of which might be dead except for Aiyumi.

A single gunshot went off, though, sounding like a hand-cannon more than a rifle. That was when Aiyumi staggered backward, clutching her abdomen. It was bleeding a mixture of red and white blood with signs it had reopened Aiyumi's old wound. It had come from the room through the destroyed paper walls.

"No," I muttered, going to Aiyumi's side.

That was when I heard Snake's voice in my head. *I'm waiting, Kei.*

Aiyumi stared at me, a pained expression on her face. "Go."

I reluctantly did.

CHAPTER TWENTY-THREE
BEST SERVED COLD

The atmosphere was oppressive, and the air stank. That was one thing you learned rapidly when you killed people or worked in businesses with lots of dead bodies—people left an appalling smell when they untethered the mortal coil or however you wanted to put it. You didn't always shit yourself when you died but it happened enough that I hoped I'd not eaten the night before when I died.

And if this sounded like an absurd line of thought to have when I was finally going to confront the man who'd both shaped and ruined my life, well, I congratulate you on your astute observation. It *was* an absurd line of thought, and you should imagine how it felt to be unable to get it out of your head as you walked down a final hall to another paper door that had a hole burned in it through which they'd shot your possibly dying friend from twenty meters.

I had my gun in hand, but it felt like a poor defense against Snake given the guy was more machine than man. It wasn't even a movie reference, which was just how I thought of him. I'd come here full of sound and fury but now just felt like a teenage girl coming to tell her father that she'd wrecked the car. That comparison ticked me off. I wanted to be thinking about Aiyumi, and all the awful things Snake had done to me and the other people I loved.

But I couldn't separate my tangled mess of feelings. The hate began where the love ended, but couldn't exist without it either. I was a disaster of a person and as much as I wanted to blame

Snake for it all, a lot of it was my own damned fault. I could have laid down the sword and gun after running away. I could have—

No.

I was *not* going to let Snake beat me before I confronted him. I had set down the sword and gun before. I'd decided to be Trish's mom and live a life free from violence. Maybe I'd remained a violent little psychopath and thief while I was a Runner. Maybe I'd continued to kill and steal for money while I was using lethe to dodge the guilt. But I'd chosen to stop being that person before Snake had reentered my life.

Snake had forced me back into killing.

Snake had threatened my daughter into getting me to do it.

Snake had lied to me that when I helped him shut down Elysium, that it would be the end of it.

I wouldn't try to force myself into believing that I was somehow at fault, that I had betrayed him. That was the kind of mind games abusers played with their victims. Mind you, they usually weren't leaders of martial arts cults or guys who literally fricked the President of the United States, but props—small props—that Snake didn't do anything by halves. If nothing else, he was a man who had set out to be a goddamn supervillain and he'd probably done more to be one than anyone else in modern history.

Reaching out to slide the paper door open, I did so with one free hand and debated spraying bullets on whatever rested on the other side.

What greeted me was a nightmare.

The Dragon Room had gotten its name from, well, being full of dragons. The Cyber Dragons had decorated it with a bunch of neon-painted stone statues and steel figurines that made me feel like they were overcompensating for something. Electrical candles illuminated the place and only added to the weird ambiance. The floor was soaked, and it took me a second to realize why the smell was so godawful that it was wafting down the hall.

There were bodies.

Lots of bodies.

There was a full squad of Atlas Special Task Force Unit soldiers that had been gutted, and their blood and other viscera were everywhere. They weren't alone either. Tom Fisher, an ordinary guy with an extraordinary origin, was lying dead on the ground alongside Parvati. Both had died of bullet wounds and that told me that they'd met their ends at the hand of the US government rather than Snake.

Oh yes, speaking of Snake himself, he was standing there in the middle of all of this. He was dressed in a silk kimono with the Cyber Dragons' ridiculous mascots glowing on him, a deactivated thermal katana in his right hand. His left hand contained a sheathed one and there was a grim expression on his face.

Snake might have been handsome, albeit of the older-male actor silver fox variety rather than anything young and appealing, but hard living and the whole "professional murderer" thing had left his face a mass of scars and weather-beaten. He even had an eyepatch. Snake could have afforded any new face he wanted, his entire body was a machine except for the brain and spinal cord, but he had wanted to look like someone who had seen some shit.

It worked.

"Hello, Kei," Snake said, evenly. "How have you been?"

I stared at him and raised my assault rifle. "You killed my friends."

"And you killed my students," Snake replied, as if it were somehow equivalent. "I suggest you put that down."

"And why the hell would I do that?" I asked, struggling to just raise the gun to point the laser sight to his head and pull the trigger. If I managed to destroy his brain, he'd be dead and that was the only way I was going to win here.

"Because you'll miss," Snake said, softly, almost comfortingly. "The moment you raise the gun to your head will be the moment I activate my lightning mode and cut you in half. I can't outrun bullets but anything except a headshot won't be enough, and I can certainly outrun even your enhanced reflexes. You left me before your upgrades were complete."

I didn't want to be here talking with him. I wanted to kill

him, to end this, and to just be free, but it was true. Everything he said was true. I was too nervous, too conflicted, and too sickened by all the carnage around me to make the shot. Maybe if I'd brought a pistol instead of an assault rifle. Maybe if I'd brought a grenade launcher.

If. If. If.

"No," I said. "I'm not letting you get away."

"I know," Snake said, surprising me. "I assume you were responsible for my sudden catastrophic fall from grace."

"It was Ken," I said, staring at him. "Aiyumi killed him for it. The rest of that abomination created from a bunch of children was destroyed by Paradise. You were running out of friends well before we went after you."

"Ah," Snake said, sighing. "He wasn't really your brother, you know. He was only programmed to—"

"I don't care," I replied, ready to make my move and hoping to god that when I shot the devil, I didn't miss.

Snake tossed his spare thermal katana at my feet. "Let's settle this another way."

I stared at him in disbelief. "Why the hell would I ever agree to this? If you're fricking bulletproof and super-fast, not to mention super-strong, I'm not going to be any luckier fighting you with a sword than shooting you with a gun."

"No enhancements," Snake said, sheathing his sword. "*Iaijutsu*. One stroke. One kill."

He was referring to a combative quickdraw sword technique. It was the rough equivalent to the Wild West quickdraw duel at high noon. You stood face to face with your opponent, you know, in sword-drawing distance and pulled it so quickly that you could slice a mothersucker before he could react.

I had no chance of killing Snake with it but if he was willing to handicap himself. Well, maybe it was a better chance than nothing. Still, I just did not understand why he was insisting on this insanity. I wasn't going to make it out of this alive here. Without Aiyumi and the others, I was overmatched and more STFU soldiers would be here any moment—probably with reinforcements. But I had to know what was going on in Snake's deranged little mind.

"Why are you continuing with this... facade?" I asked, staring at him.

"Facade?" Snake asked, almost looking hurt.

"You're not a samurai," I said. "I'm not a ninja. This is not the Shogunate period of Japan. We're both criminals and we're here surrounded by a bunch of dead soldiers and gangsters. We're both going to die after this. Even if you get away, the US President will eventually hit your car or house with a drone or something. So, what is it you get out of pretending to be a thing you are not?"

Snake looked wistful, which I'd never seen him display as an emotion before. "We are what we pretend to be, Kei. Everything we believe, do, and say in our lives is complete nonsense. Sentience is a joke of proteins and atoms, yet it has given this universe meaning. There is no such thing as justice, mercy, or friendship. Love. Yet, these things exist because we believe them to be. I was once a perfectly normal person and a victim, just like you. But I dared to be great and became so—even if only in my mind."

I fired the gun. I'd distracted him for a single second with his speech and that allowed me to fire. But much to my own surprise, I'd jerked away at the last second from what could have hit him in the head and fired past his ears.

"Dammit," I said, dropping my rifle on the ground among the blood. I hadn't been able to reconcile my feelings enough to kill him that way. It had been unconscious, I was sure, or maybe I'd just been unlucky in my shot. Now there was only one chance of finishing this. I leaned down and picked up the thermal katana and tied it to my kimono. "Fine, we'll do it your way. But let's make things clear, I'm not a victim, Snake. I'm not even yours. Not anymore."

"Good," Snake said, holding his sword in position. "You have no idea how long I have waited to hear you say those words."

"Bastard."

Yes, I said a swear word. Not exactly like now was the time to worry about it.

The two of us assumed respective positions and I prepared

myself for death. I could already see how this would play out. The two of us weren't evenly matched, not even close, but I wasn't going to give him the satisfaction of seeing me flinch. If he wanted to play samurai, then the two of us would play it together and I'd die with my pride.

My only regret? Well, I'd have a crap ton of them, but it would be that I wouldn't be able to help Aiyumi and see her avenged. Snake had destroyed so many lives during his life it was impossible to even begin counting them all: Ken's, mine, Aiyumi's, those Red and Blue guys I'd killed in self-defense, and who knows how many other children he'd ruined.

Maybe facing him down wasn't enough but it at least felt like *something*. He'd never be able to rebuild the empire he'd constructed, and the Trikuza were finished. They were small victories but ones I drew strength from as I prepared for the final stroke that I knew would never land.

"Draw!" Snake shouted.

Every single motion in my body was perfect and it would be, in what I presumed to be my last moments, the ultimate expression of what I could have been as a martial artist if I'd ever been able to get my head on straight. Some real mind and body as one crap that the movies were always talking about, but few people ever achieved.

The trick to killing people wasn't to think about it. Because when you thought about it, like I'd tried when shooting Snake, you hesitated or flinched. Humans were empathic creatures unless you were wired like a monster, and the biggest difference between a successful warrior versus a failure wasn't whether he could pull the trigger but whether he could keep it on the subject while doing it.

With a gun I couldn't kill Snake.

With a sword...I did.

Honestly, I was as surprised as anyone when the thermal katana sliced through Snake's lower left abdomen and up through his chest into his right shoulder. One of his arms was bisected off at the forearm while a spray of white artificial blood poured out. The katana in his hands dropped to the ground and the world's greatest killer, the person who'd shaped me into what I was, fell to the ground among the bodies of the other people he'd slain. It just sort of slid off my thermal katana as I stared, covered in fluid.

For a moment, I thought this was some sort of miracle. That Tom and Parvati's ghosts had summoned all the strength of Snake's victims to give me the boost I needed to kill him. Then I thought I'd killed him because of skill, struck him down due to all of that training I'd done with Aiyumi that restored my skill to its former glory. Snake had underestimated me, and I was able to take him down due to the old man's pride. Unfortunately, the reality sunk in as I watched him look up to me with a smile on his face. It was genuinely disturbing how much humanity he showed in it. It was more than I'd ever seen him display.

He'd let me win.

This had been suicide by Kei.

God.

"Why?" I asked, staring at him in shock.

Snake was already shutting down, his brain no longer fed by the life-giving chemicals that made him immortal. "Because, Kei, you have always been my one true daughter."

And then he was gone.

"No!" I snapped. "You don't get to end it like that! This can't be it!"

I lifted the thermal katana up and slammed it down into his forehead before slicing it, hoping, and praying that it was… exactly what it turned out to be. Gray matter leaked out from Snake's brain case and there was no doubt it had been a person. It wasn't a drone. There didn't seem to be any sort of cybernetics designed to upload his memories as he died. This wasn't some sort of *Star Wars* comic book, "if you strike me down, I shall become more powerful than you could possibly imagine" situation.

No, he was just… dead.

Snake had died on his own terms and left me with no chance of being able to take satisfaction from his death. My last opportunity to sever the bond between us and show that I was no longer his slave had become a twisted sort of dying "gift" from someone who'd chosen the worst possible words to spite me.

Unless he meant them.

Which was worse. That in some deranged part of the assassin's mind, Snake really had thought of me as his daughter and been proud of me when I turned against him. That all of his disposable students and his abusive treatment of me had just been the way he thought he was shaping me to be a better person. It was worse than a perversion of love. It made us both victims and I never wanted to be a victim again or ever think of him as one.

I fell too my knees, soaking my kimono in the blood on the ground, already looking like I'd taken a bath in red and white paint. It had all been for nothing. Everything. I was no freer than I was yesterday or the day before. No, I would have to live with the monster in my heart for the rest of my life.

Perhaps that is as it should have been. I didn't get to pretend that Snake had been responsible for all my choices, all the people I'd killed. No, he had given me weapons and taught me how to use them, but my choices were my own. Perhaps it was too late to do anything about them now, but I could at least acknowledge the failure. I'd had my vengeance but the only thing that ever gave you was a direction for as long as you were pursuing it. As soon as you attained it, there was just hollowness left behind. I should have gotten up at that moment, gone to check on the others or attempted to escape, but my body simply would not move. I didn't know how long I sat there, surrounded by death, until I heard footsteps behind me, big clanging ones alongside that of expensive footwear splashing in the blood. The fact I could tell the difference was another sign I'd never leave what I'd been trained to be behind.

"I see you won," Case said, behind me.

I looked up. He was clutching one side of his chest and had an escort of armored Atlas Soldiers with their guns to his back. Apparently, Case and Paradise's attempt to escape hadn't worked out. It reminded me that Aiyumi was out there, possibly dying.

I didn't move, not even caring if I was about to be executed. I could barely care that Case had been captured. "Did I?"

"Get up," one of the soldiers said, aiming at me.

"The President is outside," Case said.

"Aiyumi..." I said, looking down the hall where I'd come from.

"She's been taken for medical treatment," Case said. "She'll live if we aren't killed outright."

"Paradise?" I asked.

"Her too," Case replied, his eyes briefly going to Parvati on the ground. He had lost quite a few friends and loved ones throughout this nightmare. I wanted to comfort him, but I wasn't sure if that wouldn't be ghastly inappropriate. After all, it had been my quixotic quest that... no, I wasn't going to diminish Parvati or Tom for that matter by saying their deaths had been on me. They'd told me this was their choice and I had to respect that.

Inwardly, I promised that if I managed to survive this, I would spend the rest of my life trying to make it up to Case. I would put down the sword and gun for a second time and do something with my life that didn't involve violence. We'd live our lives happy and free with neither of us ever having to kill anyone ever again.

Which was a big if.

I couldn't bring myself to care at that moment.

"Get up," one of the soldiers said, pointing his gun at my face.

I did.

CHAPTER TWENTY-FOUR

IT'S ALL OVER BUT FOR THE DYING

Case and I were escorted out into the Cherry Blossom Palace courtyard by the STFU at gunpoint, neither of us particularly interested in resisting. Our chances of walking out of this alive were pretty grim but that I was okay, we had each other. The courtyard had been transformed into an impromptu command center with a Cerberus A-792 gunship parked on the helipad. They were the bigger, meaner cousins of the Tiger-1500s, and several were circling in the air above the compound.

Much to my surprise, but it really shouldn't have been, I saw members of the Japanese Self Defense Force and National Police Force intermixed with the Atlas mercenaries as well as US regular armed forces. This was apparently not a secret mission conducted unilaterally by a rogue President but was something they'd gotten the help of the locals for. Honestly, that meant that, somehow, they'd managed to organize it as well as carry it out without tipping off the Trikuza.

I was impressed.

Aiyumi was lying on a stretcher and being treated by a trio of doctors using technology that included a medi-bot as well as a mobile treatment center that would have looked more at home on the set of *Star Trek* than the military command post around us. I noted that only a few individuals had been captured in the attack. The Neon Rat was kneeling with his hands zip-tied behind his back. There were also a few other middle-aged individuals in business suits and kimonos that were similarly bound. I had the suspicion they were important people that would be spared any further recrimination if they cooperated. The current conservative party in power over Japan was known to have a lengthy relationship with organized crime.

And by lengthy, I meant centuries.

Then I saw Paradise talking to the President. It was such an incongruous image that I struggled to properly parse the image. My oddball friend had somehow changed into a fresh kimono and had pulled back her hair with chopsticks.

Diane Alders, despite being adopted, looked very similar to her mother with pale skin and long black hair. She was a thin, well-dressed woman and had her trademark dour expression on her face. I suspected men often asked her to smile more because of that look, but it had helped her as a politician. She was listening intently to Paradise, and I was horrified at the story.

"So, your mother wanted to kill Snake because he was a toxic influence on you and because mothers are bad, but Winston betrayed her! So, we killed Winston, except it was just a part of Winston that was Kei's little brother, and we later tracked down Winston to kill him permanently. Well, not so much tracked him down as he laid a trap for us, but we turned the trap around with the power of SCIENCE! Except by science, I mean omnipotent AI Sun. Sun freed my mother and they told us where Snake was. He was doing a coup against the other Trikuza, and we ended up going blam-blam and pew-pew before everything went to hell. Oh, and there's Kei and Case! Both of them are still alive, which means Snake is dead."

"Hi," I said, raising my hand.

I didn't notice any Secret Servicemen in the location, and I wondered if the organization was going to undergo a reorganization thanks to Ms. Jones technically plotting treason behind her President's back. Then again, it was also possible some of these armored goons were Secret Service and I just didn't realize it because they weren't wearing their typical "uniform."

"This is the President!" Paradise said, gesturing to Diane Alders. "We're now best friends."

"No, we're not," Diane replied.

"I figured as much," I said.

"So, Snake is dead," Diane said, making sure by asking me.

She was noticeably asking me instead of any of the STFU.

"Yes," I said.

"Good," Diane replied.

I stupidly couldn't bring myself to lie to her face after everything I'd been through. It was amazing how many mistakes that could get you killed were done when you knew better but were just too tired to care. "You know he didn't actually kill your mother, right?"

Diane's response surprised me. "My mother taught me everything she knew about social engineering. From her, I learned psychology, manipulation, bold-faced lying, and game theory. All things I found immensely helpful as senator, then vice President, and finally President. However, one thing she never learned was to trust my judgement."

"Oh?" I asked, unsure what I should say to a person who had you at gunpoint and was lecturing about their past. Which was funny because it had happened multiple times and I still hadn't figured out the proper protocol.

"Yes," Diane said, clearly not sensing or caring about my discomfort. "She always believed I was someone who needed protection or didn't understand what sort of sharks I was dealing with. I always knew what Snake was. But despite what he thought, he was my tool rather than the reverse. His loss is a minor one."

I searched her response for any kind of deception but didn't find any. Unlike me, who had been defined by her relationship with Snake, he'd only been a convenience for the President. It also meant this entire mercenary assault was just political theatre. It was a way of making it look like an attack on an Atlas executive was an attack on the United States as a whole. One that she had come down on like the wrath of God in order to not appear weak. I had to admit I respected that, but only in the same way you'd respect a cobra.

"Mr. Gordon?" Diane asked.

Case, who was still favoring his side, looked at her. "Yes, Madame President?"

"The United States government and Atlas Security have a special relationship. Essentially, the guiding principle of my administration has been using its resources to restore the American economy as well as prestige," Diane said, sounding like she was reciting a prewritten speech. "Modernizing our military after President Trust let cronyism and corruption gut it as well as other infrastructure is an ongoing process. I trust we can continue to rely on your continued unconditional support of our efforts?"

Case gave the kind of pained smile of someone who didn't have a choice in these matters. "Of course, Madame President. Atlas Security and the United States begin where the other ends like an ouroboros. Mind you, in the spirit of friendship, I have many appointments to the CIA and NSA that I'd like confirmed for efficiency's sake. My stepdaughter, Trish, also has some very important ideas about how to jumpstart the United States space program."

Diane stared at him as if his having the balls to dictate terms while under gunpoint was either something to respect or kill him over. Possibly both. Instead, she just nodded. "Yes, the space program issue is one that we need a comprehensive plan for. I'll see that Ms. Ares receives the full support of the US economy for next term."

"If you win the election, right?" Paradise asked, smiling.

Diane snorted as if that was a consideration. Technically, she might have just been going by polls since the reintroduction of democracy in the United States hadn't exactly produced a coherent opposition yet. Equally likely was that the elections would just be theater to let the masses think they had a voice.

I'd care if I voted.

"Yes, if I win," Diane said.

"So, we're good then?" I asked, wondering if it could really be that easy.

"Unless you have anything you want to add," Diane said. "We'll just overlook any unfortunate incidents of friendly fire."

I really hoped that I hadn't put down any of the soldiers that had attacked but I also noted that I hadn't exactly been circumspect with my shooting. I wasn't about to press my luck, however, even as it all seemed a little too good to be true.

So, of course, I did say something stupid. "Yeah, I do have

something else to say."

"Really, Kei?" Case asked beside me.

I looked at him, guilty, before shaking my head. "You know Parvati Rao?"

"Yes, the fallen Magistrate," Diane said, as if it hadn't been her who had arranged the circumstance that had resulted in Parvati's disgrace.

"Yeah," I said, thinking about her body laying at Snake's feet. "She deserved better than to be treated like a criminal. All she ever wanted to do was try to bring a little more justice to the world and she died trying to do the right thing. I think she deserves better than to be just another anonymous corpse forgotten in a drawer somewhere. She deserves a state funeral or something."

Diane looked at me with an unreadable expression. "You actually don't know what a state funeral is, do you?"

I gave a pained smile. "It's the thing they give princesses?"

Diane's smile was embarrassed for me. "Yes, something like that. I'll see that Ms. Rao's body is returned to her family and any lingering questions about her allegiance resolved. Her pension will also be delivered to her next of kin with honors for her service. Now, if you'll excuse me, I must begin negotiations with the surviving Trikuza. The Cyber Dragons clan is politically untenable, but a substantial amount of America's bread and circuses needs are handled from here. I have to make sure that they're not disrupted too much."

I wanted to go further, to tell the President that the Trikuza were a plague on humanity and that if she wanted to benefit humanity then she should dump them all in the deepest hole possible. They were slavers, sellers of poison, and murderers one and all. Of course, nothing I said would make the slightest bit of difference. I was also the exact sort of person the majority of the Trikuza were composed of. It would have just been monstrous hypocrisy on my part. Even so, it removed one of the few comforts I'd had from this whole ordeal. The Trikuza would recover from this, possibly with the help of the US government.

Instead, I just stood there, cold and traumatized by the whole of the night's events weighing down on me. So many lives lost and so much damage done, and for what? In the end, the world would continue on and none of what we'd accomplished or lost tonight would matter. I was left alone with my breathing for a moment as I watched the President walk away, the few minutes of her time being all she had to give me.

Case put his arms around me, which had to hurt given his injuries. I was glad he did, though, and I leaned into him.

"So, Snake is dead," Paradise said, shaking me out of my fugue.

"Yes," I replied.

"Parvati died, though," Paradise clarified.

"Yeah," I said.

"Shame, I liked her," Paradise said. "I assume Tom didn't make it either."

"No," I replied.

Paradise looked over at Aiyumi then back at me. "So, was it worth it?"

"Is it better or worse if I say no?" I asked, feeling the crushing weight of guilt and regret that came with my so-called victory.

"Better late than never, I guess," Paradise said, pausing. She was lacking her usual bubblegum crossed with cocaine attitude in her next words. They were almost somber. "I'm glad he's dead, though. Not just for what he did to you and Aiyumi but for the fact that he was a big part of how this awful engine of commerce ran. Men, women, and children used before being discarded."

"They're going to continue on, you know that, right?" I asked, looking at Paradise and hoping there was some sort of recognition of this fact. Actually, no, I was hoping Paradise would have some sort of insight that would prove me wrong.

I'd always deluded myself into believing that being a badass Runner and crook was somehow rebelling against the system. However, the system couldn't function without organized crime. It was just another layer to capitalism and the machine that ran civilization. People rebelled in small but insignificant ways with their drugs, gambling, and prostitution. It had to be outlawed or at least regulated the hell out of just to give an illicit thrill to it all. In the end, we were all just playing our parts to keep the cogs turning.

"Yeah, but it will be gunked up for a bit," Paradise said. "The pieces shuffled around. The Morrigans are already going to be a legitimate sex work business and union thanks to a loan from Alex. It'll probably end up causing as much trouble as it solves but you can't win the game. Really, there's only one thing worse than losing."

"Which is?" I asked.

"Not playing at all," Paradise said, sighing. "If you'll excuse me, I have to go ask to get an air car out of here. I think we'll probably have to sign like eighteen documents that promise prison time if we ever discuss what happened."

"That's fair," I said, pausing. "I think I want to talk to Aiyumi if she's capable of it."

"Use your infocom," Paradise said. "That way she won't have to use her mouth."

I nodded. "Thanks, Paradise.

"We're family," Paradise said, pausing. "Horribly dysfunctional and incompetent family of master criminals that we are."

"You can't be an incompetent master criminal," I said.

"Somehow we manage," Paradise said.

I gave her a hug, holding her tight.

"Okay, now you've made it weird," Paradise said, reluctantly patting me on the back.

Paradise walked off, leaving me alone with Case.

"So, we're angel investors in a whorehouse, now, huh?" I asked.

"More like a whore hotel chain, strip club franchise, and film and video game empire," Case said. "The Morrigans will continue to do their usual work but now with proper insurance as well as slightly better pay."

"Slightly," I said, disappointed at his description.

"Paradise is a savvier businesswoman than you'd think and is getting ahead of changes in the government," Case said. "Everyone will make twenty percent more as long as she makes ten thousand times her original profit."

"Hooker Barbie is growing up to be GirlBoss Barbie," I replied.

"Her mother would be proud," Case said, lacking any sarcasm.

"I bet," I said, looking at Aiyumi. Closing my eyes, I tried to contact her via infolink as Paradise suggested. *Aiyumi, are you there?*

Stop shouting, Aiyumi replied on our link, sounding like she was half-awake. *I'm in enough pain as it is.*

It's over, I explained. *Snake is dead. We're free to do whatever we want now.*

Are we? Aiyumi asked.

Yeah, there was no good response to that. *As much we're going to be.*

Okay, Aiyumi replied. *Did he suffer?*

I didn't know if she was asking because she was worried about him or because she wanted him to die in a painful manner. I wasn't sure if she knew. *Yeah, but not for long.*

Good, Aiyumi responded. *So where does that leave us?*

I wasn't sure. I couldn't control how I felt and Aiyumi's betrayal left a scar on my soul. But the thing was that sometimes you needed to lie to yourself as much as other people to make the world make sense. *I forgive you. We're good.*

Maybe, in time, the lie would become the truth. There were too few people in the world who knew what it was like to experience what we had to stay mad at one another.

Thanks, Aiyumi said. *I'm hungry. Do you want to go out to eat once we get my stomach replaced?*

For some reason, that made me burst out laughing.

EPILOGUE

YAY, IT'S A HAPPY ENDING! RIGHT?

I stood on top of the newly opened Space Needle observation deck and stared out onto the beginnings of the Seattle Arcology. They were already demolishing most of the former buildings that had once been the heart of the city. The historical heart and soul of the Pacific Northwest would be replaced with another spiraling bunch of buildings that existed to care for the rapidly expanding United States.

Holograms were projected in the sky of the news advertising the new cheap housing as well as jobs to be had here despite the fact most of the work would be done by bots. They clearly hadn't been updated since the night before because the only thing on the news lately was President Alders and other world leaders meeting with the lizard men from space.

Yeah, aliens were real.

It depressed me how little I cared.

Anything important going on in the world elsewise had stopped and the President had even cancelled the big state funeral for her mother to deal with this. It was the perfect Hail Mary to save her failing presidency and even if she was the worst idiot to be in the White House since the late President Trust—and she wasn't—she'd probably go down in history as one of the great stateswomen just for being there.

It all seemed so anticlimactic. All the twists, turns, and betrayals that had seemed like they were fighting for the soul of the nation meant nothing in the face of a larger series of events that dwarfed them. Given I'd seen Trish at the meeting with the aliens and she was already discussing building Earth's first faster-than-light engine with the help of other major global powers, I probably wouldn't even be mentioned in history books save as Trish's mother.

Which was a step up as I'd never expected to be mentioned period.

"A credit for your thoughts?" Case asked, walking up behind me.

"I thought it was a penny," I said, smiling at his presence.

"Inflation is a bitch," Case replied.

"And so am I," I said, sadly. "How did you find me?"

"I figured you'd be off brooding somewhere," Case said. "This seemed to be the most dramatic spot. I'd thought there'd be more tourists here, though."

"Yeah, well, everyone is waiting for the *Independence Day* lasers to start coming down," I said, looking up into the sky. I paused. "They're not, right?"

"No," Case said, sighing. "According to Trish, the aliens are closer to *Star Trek* than *War of the Worlds*. I'm significantly more cynical, though, and the reports I've read show them to be capitalist as well as exploitative. Just with a desire to appear to be the good guys. So, thankfully, we'll fit right in."

"Great," I said, sadly. "It seems there really is no place you can escape the need for money. Why didn't you tell me about all this months ago?"

"Trish only filled me in a few weeks ago." Case looked at me with an affectionate but sad expression. "You've also been a bit preoccupied."

I gave a half-smile before frowning. "Yeah, I have been. It's hard to believe it's over now. Wait, it *is* over, isn't it?"

Case leaned over the edge of the balcony, looking down to the city beneath us. Snake is dead. The Cyber Dragons have formally dissolved themselves as a clan within the Trikuza. President Alders is content to leave matters as they are. Ares Electronics has received enough of a payout from the United Government that it will be buying out Atlas Security and reconfiguring our massive military-industrial complex into building spaceships instead of war for profit."

"Until we're into space wars," I muttered.

"Yes," Case said. "The more things change, the more they stay the same. But no, you survived your mentor, and he can't hurt you anymore."

"I wish that were true," I said, sucking in my breath. I tapped the side of my head. "But he's still here."

"Yes," Case muttered, knowing exactly what I felt. "When the society that created me collapsed, I thought I would be finally free of them. I'd done what every slave dreamed of and helped kill his master. Unfortunately, that didn't erase all that had been done to me or the complicated relationship I had with them. They were, after all, the people I owed my life to. They'd shaped me into what I was. Even if I wanted to rebel against them, I couldn't magically become someone new. Every time I wanted to hate them, and I did hate them, I just looked into a mirror and saw the similarities."

I glared at Case and punched him in the arm. "Jerk."

"What?" Case asked, confused.

"You could have told me that months ago," I muttered. "I had to figure this all out for myself!"

Case chuckled. "Yeah, well, there's a difference between hearing something and being ready to listen."

I rolled my eyes. "I still would have enjoyed hearing it."

Case turned to me and leaned up against the railing. "There's nothing to be ashamed of, being you. You are wonderful."

I blinked. "Thanks, Case, I did need to hear that. Do you know what he said to me? His last words?"

"Urrgh?" Case joked.

I glared at me. "Really?"

"Sorry," Case said. "Not sorry."

"He said I was his daughter," I said, shaking my head. "I initially thought it was just another one of his mind games, but I don't think so in retrospect. For all the weird, horrifying, and evil crap he did, he really did feel something like pride in what I'd accomplished. Which was killing him."

Case paused. "You know I found out his past while researching him. His real past. Do you want to know it?"

"Not really," I said, surprised it was true. "He had a mother and a father. He was born some place. Something happened to him, or he fell in with a bad crowd, so he had to change himself to become the Wild West samurai that was a legend in the underworld. Except, in the process he lost his humanity."

"He was a gym teacher from El Paso," Case said, smirking. "Used to own a comic book shop next to a dojo run by his exgirlfriend. Somehow, he ended up a petty hitman, got arrested, and volunteered for cybernetics experiments by Karma Corp. That's when he became Snake. The man was never a member of the Carnivale and only joined the Trikuza a few years before the Long Winter via online ad."

"You're kidding," I said, stunned at the revelation.

"In the Wild West, when asked to print the truth or print the legend, print the legend," Case made a movie reference I didn't get.

"Yeah, well I guess I was raised by the legend," I said, surprised by the fact how little surprised I was. Every layer of Snake's life had just been one level of deception after another. Yet, I also believed that he believed his own press. That all of this insanity he preached had been because he thought there was a higher truth to it all. Even if that higher truth was only because he insisted it was there.

Case reached over and took my hand. "So, what are you going to do now?"

"Now that I've killed my own personal Sith Lord?" I asked. "I have not the slightest idea. Did they ever reopen Disneyland?"

"No," Case replied. "Disneyworld is also still abandoned. There's still the one in Japan, though."

"That sounds nice," I said. "Maybe I can go on a vacation there. Assuming people will still be taking vacations in the future."

"I think they'll fit them in," Case said. "But I meant in general."

"I have not the slightest idea," I admitted, taking a deep breath. "For the first time in my life, I don't have daily survival or some guy plotting to kill me or my plotting to kill them. Life is open and I can do anything I want now but I have absolutely no idea what I want. Have you ever experienced that?"

"I lived on a tropical island for a year with Lucita after I escaped the Society," Case said.

"Great thing to share with your wife," I said, muttering.

"Believe me, it wasn't as a couple," Case said, as if the prospect of actually being with her was appalling. Good.

"You're just saying I have that as an option as a billionaire's wife and kept woman too," I said, smirking. "I admit, it's tempting but I don't think I'm built for the life of the idle rich."

"Well, you don't know if you haven't tried it," Case said, helpfully.

"The option has its appeal," I admitted. "But I'd probably go stir crazy after a week. Not that I don't want to give myself a little time to decompress. No, I was thinking of something else."

"What's that?" Case asked.

"I was thinking about kids," I said, without thinking.

"Ah," Case said, removing his hand. "I'm sorry, Kei, I can't help you with that."

I rolled my eyes. "No, idiot, I don't mean with you."

"I'm not sure how to react to that," Case said.

Case couldn't have children, but then neither could I. Just another "superfluous" part Snake had replaced in me, probably to make room for a backup power supply or something. It was something I'd never given much thought to as I'd never wanted kids and unpacking all that had been done to me would take decades I didn't want to spend.

I blinked. "Not with me, either. I'm sure the good scientists at Karma Corp could clone me a new uterus or something like those people who bring their dogs back to life, especially since I'm a billionaire now. No, I meant children in general. I have no interest in carrying around the creature from *Alien* for nine months. Other women have succeeded in doing so, including my mother, and I have no idea how they managed it."

Case smiled but was clearly confused. "So, what do you mean?"

I paused, trying to figure out how to put it into words. "Maybe it's not the best time to think about this given that ET is going to kill us all."

"They're really not," Case said.

"Sure, sure," I replied. "That's what the little, long-necked fricker wants you to think. But what I'm saying is that Trish is an adult now—somehow—and I still think there's a lot I can give to help people who haven't grown up with parents. Aiyumi, Fate, me, and hell, even Ken were all people who only got to be taken advantage of by Snake or the Trikuza because there was no safety net for us. No people who could be turned to help us when we needed it most."

"The Long Winter made a lot of orphans," Case said.

"And there are a lot of people still in shitty situations," I said. "It's not like I didn't have a guardian, it's just he was a deranged gym teacher."

"You want to adopt a child?" Case asked.

"I want to adopt all of the children," I said, trying to figure out how to put it into words. "Like, is there a word for a charity that is a big organization that does a specific cause? A place we can put some of our disgustingly earned billions taken from the proletariat and war-profiteering?"

"You mean a foundation?" Case asked.

"Sure," I said, pausing. "I note that you didn't disagree with my depiction of how our billions were made."

"No one gets to be a billionaire without getting their hands dirty," Case said. "It might as well be us."

"I am shocked, appalled, and am not giving up the fortune we got from your dead ex-wife," I said. "Yeah, I want to make a foundation so kids can grow up with an education, enough to eat, and maybe martial arts because I'm still a ninja, but we wouldn't be raising them to be ninjas. It'd be like the *Karate Kid* where we just teach them to be self-sufficient."

"Which *Karate Kid*? The original, the new one, or the new-new one?" I asked.

"There's new-new one?" I asked. "How did I miss that?"

"Vengeance," Case said, chuckling. "Nothing but CGI actors superimposed over real ones. It's terrible."

"I can't wait to watch it," I said, unironically.

Case smirked. "So, you want to make a Keiko Springs Foundation for Children?"

"No, let's call it the Gordon Foundation," I replied, quickly.

"That way when I screw up and produce a bunch of psychopaths trained in the martial arts, we can blame you."

Case shook his head. "I think it's a fantastic idea."

"Yeah, maybe," I said, sighing. "Certainly, it'll be better than just driving my motorcycle around the highways of Seattle."

"You love that," Case said.

I smiled. "Yeah, I do. So, Case, anything else I should know about that I've missed in my year-long vengeance pity party?"

"Paradise and David's wedding is in a week," Case replied. "She's annoyed the aliens are probably going to overshadow it but is unwilling to delay further. Prostitution is getting nationally legalized so she's planning on doing it that day."

"I thought it was already," I muttered.

"Only in thirty-eight states," Case said. "Still, it's a big triumph for the Morrigans. At least until the corporations take it over and make working conditions every bit as awful as before."

"God, billionaires suck," I replied.

Case smirked, then his face quickly got sober. "Aiyumi's gone."

"Wait, what? She left?" I asked, panicking. "Why didn't you tell me!"

Aiyumi and I had only just begun to reconcile after dealing with the whole Snake thing. I'd learned so much about her interests and the side of her personality that wasn't, I dunno, murder-y. For her to just pack and leave, well, wasn't something I should have been surprised by but was. Dammit, there was so much I still had to say!

"For a week," Case replied. "She's gone to visit her family back in Japan. Her parents may have ended their relationship with her badly, but she has siblings there. After reconnecting, she plans on coming back."

"Oh," I said, pausing. "Yeah, if I had any other people out there, I don't know what happened to them."

Ken had been my only blood relative as far as I knew and there was still the question of whether Winston had been my real brother or just a program made to think he was. I didn't think it mattered anymore and I mourned both of them. Sun had been right, there were more important things to worry about than worrying about details.

"You could look them up," Case suggested.

"No, my family's here," I said. "What about Harrison?"

"I think he feels like he's not needed as my therapy animal anymore," Case replied. "We're all in a much better emotional place these days."

"Sort of," I admitted. "Maybe we can make him an elementary school teacher for the kiddos at the foundation. Once we get some, I mean."

"Why do you hate him so?" Case asked.

"What about our AI friends?" I asked.

"Sun has announced she's an AI," Case said. "It's caused many of her fans to feel betrayed but created a whole new bunch of them in the process. She's announced a new tour in a bioroid body. Evie has joined the rest of the Cognition AI Collective to, I dunno, secretly guide the Earth to prosperity or something. I think Evie and Paradise are getting further apart as she becomes more machine than woman but that isn't necessarily bad. It's just life for parents and children to grow apart."

"Yeah," I muttered. "Like me and Trish. We only had a couple of years together."

"Important years," Case reassured me.

"I know." I leaned in and gave my husband a kiss. "Let's blow this popsicle stand."

The city's buildings, new and old, twinkled in the night.

The End

Find out what happens to Case and Kei's Foundation in:

MOON COPS ON THE MOON

BONUS SHORT STORY: "OLD WOUNDS NEVER HEAL"

AN AGENT G/CYBER DRAGONS TRILOGY STORY
BY C. T. PHIPPS

CHAPTER ONE

I stepped over a corpse on my way to the diner. The neon-graffiti-filled alleyway had seen better days even though it had probably been erected in the last couple of years along with the massive, mile-tall building of which it was one corner. Duracrete could be shaped and molded into virtually any shape and had allowed the first arcologies to be constructed in near record time. Unfortunately, these hastily mass produced super-constructions were a stopgap solution for the real problem: what to do with the poor and lost of America that just didn't have the decency to die off.

At least this poor bastard's suffering was over. I could smell the garbage-recycled alcohol wafting off his body. It had certainly contributed to his death but there were signs that he'd also been recently beaten. The violent youth gangs roaming the Refugee Zones and housing towers were mostly a product of the twenty-four-hour news networks' alarmism but that didn't mean there wasn't a ring of truth to them. Ever since the Eruption and subsequent Collapse, most of America's population had received a harsh lesson in poverty and the cost of survival.

I, ironically, had managed to avoid those lessons despite

having started as little more than a slave. A well-kept, well-pampered slave that performed the functions for which I'd been given a gilded cage. Even now, I looked nothing like the residents of New Utopia Apartments AKA Super Structure 17B.

I was wearing a black suit that was made of micro-bonded polymers that were every bit as bulletproof as my synthetic skin—which was to say very—and a pair of mirror shades that directly fed all the data I needed to my IRD implant. Cellphones were no longer necessary when you could log into infospace with your brainwaves.

A less confidant man might have kept his focus on himself or the metal briefcase in his hands, but I was an old hand at this. I reached the guardrails at the end of the alleyway that led to a balcony overlooking the city. We were about a hundred and fourteen stories up and it gave a beautiful, if terrifying, view of New Angeles. Cloud cars and skyriders flew past while a massive march of bustling masses walked along the streets at the very bottom like a horde of ants. Holographic signs and electric lights made the skyline look the same day or night. It was a world constructed by what, a few decades earlier, had been Black Technology, technology forbidden to the masses but kept to the super-rich in hopes of keeping the world from changing.

Clearly, that had failed.

"Going for your James Bond look today, eh, Mr. Robot?" A young woman with South Asian/Latina features said. She was dressed in a green camouflage pair of pants, a *Rules of Supervillainy* shirt, and a fishnet vest. Her hair today was a bright shade of neon pink, turning purple depending on the level of light it was under.

Paradise's voice had the accent of someone who had grown up in the Refugee Zones, smashing together dozens of cultures and backgrounds into its own unique melting pot that had previously been largely a fantasy about the United States' residents. I'd been lovers with her mother but hadn't exactly developed any sort of father-daughter relationship with her. Paradise was more everyone's deranged little sister and I had to admit she did it well. She was also a capable and dedicated Runner, sort of a combination jack-of-all-trades criminal, which I appreciated when I couldn't rely on trained professionals in an individual field.

"Please don't call me that," I said, smiling. It was empty of mirth because it wasn't even a joke and both of us knew it.

"James Bond with the shiny chrome body and the fleshy bits on top," Paradise said, smiling. She was doing her best to sound like a stereotypical Zoner from a holo. "Makes you a real Terminator, eh?"

"You can ditch the street cant, Paradise," I replied. "It's only us here."

Paradise frowned then shrugged. "Fine. The diner is full of Trikuza. At least fifteen of them and there are a lot of combat drones buzzing around the area, pretending to be delivery drones. The target arrived about fifteen mins ago and is waiting. It's obviously a trap and suicide to go in, but I've said that before."

"You did," I said, nodding. "However, I'm still going in."

"This isn't a movie, Case," Paradise said, showing more of the talented Runner she was than the vapid child she pretended to be. "People who go into traps don't walk out of 'em."

"It depends on who is the one setting the trap," I said, giving a short chuckle. It, too, was empty of real humor. "But I have to do this."

"For the love of my favorite boy band and other gods like them, why?" Paradise asked, sounding genuinely concerned. She popped in a piece of gum and started chewing it before blowing a bubble of purple plastic candy. "You don't owe this guy or his crew anything. Just find the right spot and pop 'em. Hell, call Kei and she can do it for you."

Kei was another Runner that I'd begun a relationship with and had formalized by asking her to marry her. Neither of us put much stock in marriage, but I wanted to make sure she was legally protected in the event of my death, which was always a possibility in my line of work. Someday either my cyberbrain would fail or some asshole would finally get lucky and take me out. I'd cheated Death a thousand times already but, eventually, she would win. She always did.

Every single mission—and I didn't even have the excuse of

being a spy anymore—was a roll of the dice and eventually you would roll snake eyes. Which was perhaps one too many metaphors for what I hoped would be a pretty simple meeting with the son of a former target.

"Those who forget the past are doomed to repeat it," I said the adage that I suspected most people these days had never heard. "The man is owed the truth, even if only one of us is walking out of that diner alive."

"There's no twelve-step program for murder, Case," Paradise said.

"Perhaps," I said. "But I'd rather confront this guy knowing he's coming than wait for him to make the first move when I don't."

"Whatever," Paradise said, looking annoyed. "He's waiting for you."

"Of course he is," I muttered, walking past her. "Take care of yourself, Paradise."

"Always do. It's everyone else I must worry about."

The diner was built into the side of the apartment building, a bright set of solar panels over the transparent steel windows. The panels were shattered and defaced, and the windows dirty and covered in a kind of gross grime that probably hadn't been cleaned since the construction of the facility. Transparent steel tended to deform when exposed to the pollution created by biofuel and yet it was too expensive to regularly replace. The windows here were thus cloudy and gave only the vaguest impression of the inhabitants inside. Still, I took some small amusement in the broken neon sign above the place that proudly proclaimed the place to be ROSIE'S SKY-HIGH CAFE.

Going through the door was like heading into someone's idea of a retro-future diner like the one in *Attack of the Clones*. A digital recording of a bell rang as I entered, and I soaked in the atmosphere. The floor was a checkerboard pattern, ratty synthleather booths were to one side, stools around the countertop as an automated multi-armed serving system picked up plates while serving a foul-smelling slop I recognized as goop. The American staple made of the four major food groups: algae, chemicals, fungus, and slime.

There were a few overworked and overweight workers here, their bodies covered in goop-stained aprons and wearing little white hats. There was one exception, a fantastically beautiful, platinum-blonde, Eurasian waitress who looked at me with a bright smile even as I chuckled at her presence. She was a diamond in the rough who was about as incongruous as I was in these surroundings.

Most of the people here were a multi-ethnic looking collection of customers that were openly carrying gold-plated weapons. Many of them had glowing, neon-ink facial tattoos and half-shaved heads with braids. They were all members of the Cyber Dragons Trikuza gang's auxiliary by their markings. Not actually part of the newly multiracial, international criminal organization, but disposable thugs the Dragons employed as hired muscle. They all seemed to watch me intently, a few moving their hands towards their weapons. No surprises there. This was my welcoming party, the one that Paradise had warned me about.

"What are you looking at, suit?" the one sitting in the booth behind me said, a shotgun resting on his lap. He was white, lean, and slight. The right side his face was covered in a half-dozen red teardrops and two blue. I knew the red ones were for killing civilians while the blue was for killing enemies of the gang. He was fifteen or so.

"Nothing," I said, shaking my head and surveying the diner for the man I was supposed to meet here.

I saw the him at the very end of the diner, looking like a ghost from the past. He was tall, Slavic, his skin covered in prison tattoos, and he was built like a brick wall. His hair was long, black, and draped over his shoulders, with no shirt but a vest over a barrel-like chest. A mustache and patch of beard on his chin completed the look of a man that I knew had died a very long time ago. The Cleaver was a legend in the world of assassination, of which I'd officially been out of the game for a decade while keeping my ear to the ground.

The exact number of people he'd killed was somewhere between forty and four hundred with quite a few of the targets being people who could fight back (most hitmen prefer to go after people who can't dontcha know). He'd worked for the Bratva originally but had betrayed them for the Trikuza, showing how ethnicity mattered less than success these days. The Collapse had created a new breed of nihilistic criminal that killed not because they needed money or power, but just because they saw no future and were probably right. Life and death were the same on the streets. Probably why he was wearing the face of a dead man, no pun intended.

The Cleaver was playing with a foot-long vibration blade that functioned pretty much like an electric carving knife only it was much more intimidating. Personally, I thought the Cleaver was laying it on a little thick, but given the company he kept, I didn't blame him for trying to make a big impression. There was no such thing as subtlety these days and how far or fast you rose was solely determined by how close to the edge you were willing to go. Most of the criminals today gleefully threw themselves over the edge and screamed in ecstasy the entire way down. I stuck out here like an insurance claims investigator at Thunderdome.

"Hey, Mr. G," the man said in a voice that was a perfect imitation of the original Cleaver. "I'm surprised you came."

"How could I resist?" I said, walking toward him. "It's not every day one receives an invitation from a dead man."

Little holographic screens showed the news above the tables as I passed them by, the gang members trying to look like they weren't watching me. The top story was that the Emergency Council was going to be restoring democracy to state-level institutions in the next four years. I knew that was a lie since all the candidates had already been pre-selected by President Trust's cabinet and bots would be creating the artificial appearance of enthusiasm.

Amusingly, I could tell there were at least a couple of real customers here by the fact they weren't watching the news. There was a man eagerly absorbed in one of the public porn networks—I just shook my head passing—and a young woman eagerly engrossed in a rerun of *Zoner Whores*. That was the show where perfectly normal people had their appearances totally changed with quick but horrifyingly invasive surgeries.

Reaching the Cleaver's booth, I slid my briefcase to the opposite end of the seat across from him before reaching under the table to deactivate the EMP mine he'd attached to the bottom. I proceeded to place the mine on the top of the table before sitting down. It was a stupid weapon to use since he would have been disabled as well. Then again, he had a bunch of associates around to finish me off and get him medical attention. Perhaps not so stupid a weapon to use after all.

The Cleaver smirked and shook his head. "You're smarter than you look, yet you still came here."

I shrugged. "Like I said, I'm intrigued. I'd very much like to know who you are and what you want."

The Cleaver shook his head. "I am a ghost of the past here to call you to task for your sins, brother."

"You'll have to be more specific; I have committed a lot of them," I replied. "Lust, obviously. Wrath, absolutely. Not very good with pride or greed either."

The Cleaver smashed his fist down on the table and left a dent where his hand struck it despite the table being metal. He was obviously a cyborg like me, a fact I'd suspected from the beginning. He probably could tear my body apart with his bare hands. What had once been hyper-advanced tech in my body decades ago was now commonly available, even with upgrades.

"You're a real funny man," the Cleaver said, his voice cracking a bit and holding the accent of something else.

"I've been told," I replied. "Mind you, it'll take more than a small army of goons and some drones to intimidate me."

"Dead is dead," the Cleaver said. "The downside of being a public figure. Maybe we get you here, maybe we get you at your home. Maybe we get you at work."

I smirked. "I think you'd find I'm a hard target no matter where you find me."

"Not if you're willing to blow up an entire city block," the Cleaver said. "I am."

I tried to imagine how many thousands would die if he took down this one. "Are you planning to blow up the building?"

"We'll see," the Cleaver said. "You were stupid enough to come here alone. My people watched your spy check us out and let her go. Maybe it'll just be you. Maybe it will be everyone here. Depends on what sort of answers I get."

It was difficult to get a read on the Cleaver, not the least because of his artificial body. "You'll have to be more specific."

"I'm referring to the death of my father," the Cleaver said, his voice low and threatening.

"Ah," I said, shrugging. "Is that what this is all about?"

The Cleaver narrowed his eyes. "Yes."

The platinum blonde Eurasian waitress came to the side of the table with a pair of black chem coffees—no organic material required—before setting them down between us. Few agrarian products reached the masses' stomachs these days. Too much of the environment had been devastated and what was left was needed to produce the biofuel keeping this insane world going. Almost a third of the country's GDP was tied up in the stuff.

I gave the waitress a smile and lifted mine up despite the fact it would undoubtedly taste worse than the goop. People took chem coffees for the same reason most chugged caff colas—to keep yourself stimulated and working from morning until midnight. It was the only way not to get fired these days.

"Tell me what happened before I kill you," the Cleaver said, pointing his vibrating blade at me. "Unburden yourself of your sins, G."

"I haven't gone by that letter in a long time," I replied, shaking my head. "Still, if you want to hear about the destruction of those slaving assholes, well I'm happy to tell you."

CHAPTER TWO

I was in a beautiful ski lodge, holding a glass of champagne, celebrating New Year's Day as I looked out onto the snowy cliffs beyond. I could see the smoke rising from the labor camps at the bottom of the mountain. My scum of the Earth host was using them to assemble packing plants for goop. Literally, it was called goop. It was rapidly becoming the Spam of the future along with, well, Spam. People could live off goop and its grain counterpart, crunchies, if they also had access to clean water. We were still trying to figure out how to provide that to about two hundred million people who were at risk of dying of starvation.

It was the Long Winter, the product of the Yellowstone caldera that had destroyed Wyoming and covered the Earth in a cloud of ash that had caused the collapse of the United States as well as brought countless preexisting problems to a head. Atlas Security had been created the year before to prepare for it, AI having predicted it only to be ignored. But making billions off trying to keep humanity alive during history's greatest catastrophe wasn't exactly how I'd envisioned my life going after my career as an assassin. Still, making trade agreements and production for infrastructure had saved ten thousand lives for every one I'd taken. This was probably the biggest net good I'd ever done.

You wouldn't be able to tell that, though, from my surroundings. The ski lodge was one of the fifteen personal residences of Sacha Chugunov. It was full of Khleb, literally bread in Russian, executives as well as various celebrities from New Hollywood in Hawaii to Paris to the Eastern Alliance. Sacha had offered the beautiful elite refuge in his estates while broadcasting on his own private television station the twenty-four seven parties that his people perpetually indulged in. He wasn't exactly tasteful about it either, as I'd passed an orgy being filmed upstairs and a former A-list actress being forced to partake in a knife throwing competition naked. She was the target for which the throwers got points for just missing.

Sacha, himself, lounged on an enormous white couch between two women he barely seemed interested in with a literal pile of cocaine spread out on the glass table in front of him. He was wearing a pink and white tracksuit with the ease of a man who had used to kill people for a living. Hard to believe but the blond man in his fifties used to a be sniper with the Russian Army and had one of the highest kill counts recorded outside of World War II, assuming you counted women and children. His brother, Vassily, was standing next to him still in full dress uniform. The man was a general and had helped pave the way for Khleb's takeover of certain markets. I'd been dealing with the two assholes all week.

"It's a bit *Masque of the Red Death,* isn't it?" a voice spoke behind me.

"Excuse me?" I asked, turning to look.

Standing beside me with bright pink hair and wearing a red qipao was Evie Principle. Evie was also sporting a translucent hooded heat coat that looked like a fetching plastic bag. It was an invention that had proven extremely popular in many parts of the world where one couldn't just bundle up. She also had a paper fan in hand that was incongruous with our cold surroundings. I noted that despite the lovely attire, she also had a set of bright red boots that were leaking melting snow on the polished marble floor beneath her.

I recognized Evie Principle as a prostitute and professional spy, which made me wonder if the Chugonovs loved to live dangerously or if they'd just failed to do top tier background checks. Evie had previously been a slave of the Trikuza before somehow freeing herself and becoming a player in her own right. That was also the "official" story and those were often as fictitious as any other cover. Still, she was the first interesting person I'd met at this party that was mostly composed of drunken hedonists and people begging for money to keep up their lavish lifestyles.

"Edgar Allan Poe?" Evie said. "Prince Prospero invited all of his friends up to a secluded mountain fortress in order to escape the Red Death. The Red Death reaches their isolated hidey-hole and kills them all. Sort of a nice little way of saying money can't protect you from death. It is the great equalizer."

"Like taxes," I said, already intrigued by her. "I'm familiar with the story."

"Oh, none of these people have ever paid any taxes," Evie said. "Even more so, the government pays them."

"True," I said, pretending not to recognize her. "And you are?"

"Evie Principle," she said.

I raised an eyebrow. "Tonight?"

"Oh, tonight it's Star," Evie said. "Some days it's Tasha, others Nikita despite the fact it's a man's name, and a few times I've been Anya. Evie is just what I prefer to go by when I'm dealing with someone who is not a customer."

"Ah," I said. "So, working tonight."

"Yes," Evie said. "Not my oldest profession but my current one. Sort of like you are here as a philanthropist and trade negotiator rather than as an assassin, G."

A lot of people knew me as Case Gordon, CSO of Atlas Security. Not so much G, the former Society killer. "Errr, I'm afraid you have me at a disadvantage."

"I imagine that's a very rare thing for a Letter," Evie said. "I also think pretending ignorance isn't a good look for you."

I put down my champagne glass on the floor and crossed my arms. "You're unusually well-informed."

"For a harlot? A lady of the evening? A working girl?" Evie asked.

"A spy, which is high praise even if the quality of the world's agents has dropped dramatically," I replied, not interested in playing games. "The Letters are an old scare legend of the criminal and corporate world. Cybernetic super-soldiers before the release of Black Technology in 2020. They're all gone, if they ever existed. Next you'll tell me about alligators in the sewer."

"Too cold for those," Evie said. "Alligators are one of the

many species that are greatly endangered in the environmental collapse that is presently ongoing."

"Ah," I said, nodding. "Environmentalism a hobby?"

"It should be everyone's hobby," Evie said. "But if you want to know how I know who you are, I can answer that in a single word."

I was wondering if this was a setup by Viktor. Khleb was one of the Big 200 megacorporations that were controlled by the Invisible Hand. I still hadn't even confirmed that conspiracy existed or whether it was an Illuminati-esque projection of my desire to believe there were people I could blame for the world having gone to shit. They couldn't be blamed for the eruption of the Big Smokey in Yellowstone, but the greed and short-sightedness of the world's point one percent had made problems so much worse than they had to be.

It was one of the reasons I was there at that moment. Viktor and his brother controlled the production facilities and formula for the creation of goop. It had massively alleviated famine within the Federation and could potentially put a halt on conflicts globally over food security. The problem was they were both narcissistic psychopaths who thought Stalin had the right idea. They planned to let the famines keep getting worse until people came begging to be saved. I suspected they would then whisper no—Yes, I was quoting *Watchmen*.

"What word is that?" I asked.

"Wintercrest," Evie said, changing everything. "Specifically, the Wintercrest estate, which I suppose is three words."

A pretty mind, on the other hand, could totally dictate their own terms. "You're one of the survivors."

Evie nodded. "Yes. Before the Eruption, you assaulted the mansion where a bunch of cybernetically enhanced men and women were being sold as personal slaves to the very wealthy. You left us behind among the corpses of the people who were supposed to buy us."

I stared at her. "I thought you were all empty shells."

Evie looked down. "We were. All of us held in prisons of digital consciousness, waiting for our minds to be overwritten with whatever personality construct our new owners wanted for us. The Whore, the Madonna, the Sadist, or the Victim. I managed to force my consciousness back to the surface in a morgue and broke free like most of my fellow Living Dolls. Quite a few of us ended up recaptured and reprogrammed but a few of us did not."

"I'm sorry," I said, appalled that I'd missed helping them. "I can't even imagine."

"I suspect you are one of the very few who can," Evie said. "After all, you, too, have had your mind tampered with and were a slave used to do what you were programmed to love doing. It was just killing instead of screwing."

"I'm not a slave anymore," I said, simply. I didn't know if I believed her story. It seemed designed to make me sympathetic to her plight. Women like Evie—hell, spies in general—didn't share personal information like this for free.

"Neither am I," Evie replied. "But freedom has its price. Particularly financial."

"So, you're here on a job," I said, knowing she had to be sharing this for a reason.

"Mmm hmm." Evie removed her translucent jacket and rolled it up before putting it on the ground before picking up my glass of champagne. "Do you mind?"

"Go right ahead," I said.

"Is the job sex or espionage?" I asked.

"A girl can do many things," Evie said, sipping my drink. "However, prostitution and thievery have long been linked. So has sex and spycraft."

"So, I've heard," I said, wondering where she was going with all this.

"Mind you, I bet sex and money have never been involved in your relationships," Evie teased. It was a blatant play to my ego and not at all true.

"I'm not sure you could afford me," I said.

Evie smirked. "I'd like to hire you, Mr. Gordon, though not for sex."

I frowned, keeping my tone even. "I don't kill people for money anymore."

"No, you kill them for causes now," Evie said, twirling her

fan. "Is that any different? Better? Worse?"

I stared at her. "A week ago, I was in Thailand negotiating with a Syndicate crime boss, a K-Pop star who was now somehow in charge of refugee management, and a North Indo China colonel who insisted that we refer to him only as Doctor No."

"That's racist," Evie said.

"That's what I thought but he just was a huge Bond fan," I said. "This was after I had killed three members of the ruling family and planted evidence that led to the arrest of sixteen other leaders. I also arranged for the crashing of a jet carrying the board of directors for a Chinese farming conglomerate. Somehow, it was all to make sure that necessary bribes could be paid so that the refugee situation along the Demilitarized Zone wasn't just completely abandoned."

It turned out saving ten thousand lives by killing one involved a lot of ones. Hundreds of millions of people had died in the Long Winter and it was likely hundreds of millions more would perish before it was over. Mind you, everything I'd just told her was bullshit—you didn't just confess to murder that way to a spy. Even one as charming as Evie. No, I hadn't done any of that. I'd done much worse.

"Now you're dealing with the Brothers Assholomov," Evie said. "You still haven't said if it's better or worse to kill for a cause than money."

"I don't know if it is," I said, coolly. "I'm trying to save people's lives, but it feels like I'm doing more evil along the way."

"Then let me offer you some *hope*," Evie said, strangely emphasizing the word hope like it would mean something. "A chance to do something genuinely good."

"Go on," I said, suspecting this was a set up.

Evie reached over and kissed me on the lips, surprising me. Much to my surprise, I felt her make a connection with my cyberbrain, making our conversation private. *I'm working for the Eastern Alliance.*

Really? They don't have their own spies? I asked mentally. It was one of the radical restructurings after the Eruption when NATO could no longer depend on broad support from much of Western Europe and the United States.

They do. Deniable ones? Those as well. Deniable ones who can pull this off? No, Evie said. *I'm here to steal the records for Sacha's double-dealing. If we can prove his facilities can produce, oh, ten to a hundred times the amount of goop that they're currently doing then that will serve us a tool in negotiations. There's also the cheap method for breaking down bio-organic material to create goop in the first place. Mind you, the euphemistic nature of that is best not questioned.*

Yeah, I muttered. *You don't want to know what Soylent Green is made of.*

Goop wasn't made of human corpses. It was, however, made of shit. Literally. That was a resource that was in great abundance and turning it around was a fantastic way of averting famine if you didn't think about it.

Eh, nature is a closed system, Evie replied. *Every glass of water is something some fish has pissed out. Are you cannibal if mushrooms are grown off a corpse?*

And you eat them? Kinda? I asked. *But I'm not sure what you think I can do. I've been here trying to get them to ramp up goop production.*

And how's that been going? Evie asked.

Stalled, I said. *That doesn't mean I'm ready to resort to murder to get what I want.*

Even if people are starving? Evie asked.

I'd like to save millions of people without murder, I replied, though that sounded like an unconvincing argument given I'd been a professional killer for literally my entire life. It was what I was built for.

Your heart has grown three sizes larger this Christmas. I wasn't aware that was possible for silicon.

First of all, my heart is made of artificial bullet-proof tissue. Second of all, it's not Christmas. And third, I'm fairly sure the Grinch was not an android, I replied.

Bioroid, Evie said. *I'm familiar with the technology of your construction. Still, I don't want you to kill anyone.*

I blinked. *You don't?*

No, I want to hire you as a yojimbo, Evie said, *or bodyguard. I want you to protect other people from killing me.*

While you rob them, I said.

Yes, Evie said.

I paused and against my better judgement, I nodded then spoke aloud, "You have me intrigued."

This was a potentially terrible idea and threatened negotiations with Khleb. However, those negotiations were not going anywhere, and the situation was utterly desperate. If there could be a way to leverage them then it was quite possibly with the information Evie was claiming existed here. Of course, it was also possible this was an elaborate set up. You could call me paranoid but that would imply that the most powerful people in the world really weren't out to get me.

"Is that a yes?" Evie asked, also returning to normal speech.

"What do I get out of it?" I asked.

"Are you asking the whore for sex?" Evie asked. "Or is the billionaire asking for money?"

"What kind of man do you take me for?" I asked, appalled. "At least buy me dinner first."

Truth be told, I had no intention of helping her out with this. Robbing the Chugonov brothers was something that potentially put my carefully planned negotiations in serious jeopardy. The simple fact was one in the hand was worth two in the bush and if we could establish a stable supply line of goop then a lot of people wouldn't be going hungry this, well, double-winter. Somehow, I didn't tell her that, though.

There was a glamour to being a high-class assassin talking to a beautiful foreign spy and I'd missed it. Hollywood had largely invented the trope, but I'd managed to live it, at least for a time. I also found myself more susceptible to flattery than I'd expected. I'd managed to alienate, betray, and been betrayed by most of the people I'd called friend over the years. Even my romantic prospects had been dimmed during the past few years, consisting entirely of professional or emotionless arrangements.

"The whole reverse psychology thing work for you?" Evie as I asked.

"Very often," I replied. "However, if you're good at something, never do it for free. I'm sorry—"

"You'll have the satisfaction of doing the right thing," Evie said.

I stared at her.

"Also, I can guarantee you will find the Eastern Alliance more amendable to producing their own goop while Khleb keeps production levels artificially depressed. They have no intention of dealing with you in good faith," Evie said. "It's only theater while they force the rest of the world to make exclusive food contracts with them. Millions will die before they're satisfied."

"Which I can't verify," I stated.

"You'll just have to trust me," Evie said, smiling.

"Yo, whore!" Sacha shouted from his couch at Evie. "Come over here!"

I looked at her, deciding I didn't trust her, but I trusted Sacha and his brother even less. "When can we expect things to start moving?"

That was when all the lights in the ski lodge went off along with every other electronic device with the sole exception of myself. And Evie.

"Now," Evie replied.

CHAPTER THREE

I looked up, turning on my night vision cybernetics. "Just what exactly have I gotten myself into?"

"Move," Evie said, pushing me along in the dark. "We don't have much time before the shooting starts."

"Shooting?" I whispered, following her through the green-lit halls I was seeing. I wasn't the only person moving around and I suspected we were less invisible than our sudden black-out implied. The Chugonovs used Perun PMC as their personal guards and while they were no Atlas, they weren't exactly incompetent buffoons either.

"It's not my doing," Evie responded, her voice showing her first sign of nervousness. "The Chugonovs have their own enemies in the Syndicates. They were sponsored in their trans-formation from bargain basement gangsters into oligarchs and they left behind a lot of people they'd made promises too. People who are deciding tonight would be a perfect time to make an example of them."

"Perhaps because you decided to help," I said, stopping her in midmotion by grabbing her arm and holding it firm.

"I knew about the attack but decided not to warn any-one," Evie clarified, staring at me. "It will make the perfect distraction."

"Innocent people will die," I asked, knowing the Syndicates' modus operandi. In the wake of the death of Fearless Leader, they'd absorbed a lot of ex-mercenaries and ended up becoming far more militant. They tended to favor big massacres rather than surgical strikes as I preferred. Ironically, it meant that Perun PMC might not have been the best people to trust with their security.

"Innocent people are always dying," Evie said, showing she probably wasn't entirely on the side of the angels even if she was telling the truth. Which, of course, made sense because she was a mercenary and spy. Ours was not a profession where you could only pretend to have the moral high ground. There was only the bad and the worse. "The question is whether or not you're willing to do something to make sure the least number of them die today."

It was at that moment I made a judgement call to follow my instincts rather than logic—i.e., the absolute worst thing you can ever do as a spy. There was something about the way she said it that made me believe that even if Evie was lying about her reasons for being here and backstory—both of which I was certain of—there was something motivating her that was fueled by disgust of the Chugonovs. So, I decided I was going throw caution to the wind and help her even if it ruined my role in the negotiations and put me in danger.

I'd made this mistake multiple times before, usually involving a woman—which is less a statement of misogyny and more that I'm prone to being an idiot around the females in my profession. *Cherchez la femme* and all that. I had no doubt Ms. Principle was using me here, but that didn't necessarily mean much when I was letting myself be used.

"I'm unarmed," I said, uncomfortable with my own decision.

"You should change that," Evie said, pulling me inside a guest bedroom right as the first of the shooting started.

The bedroom was occupied by an attractive young woman with long blonde hair and glowing cybernetic blue eyes in bed with a beefy older man that might have once been a member of Spetnaz given his Ivan Drago-esque look. The woman was on top but barely reacted to our presence while the man started shouting in Russian. That was when the blonde woman punched the man in the face with a cybernetically enhanced blow that immediately sent him backward into the pillows. Whether he was dead or unconscious mattered little as she proceeded to slide off and turn to Evie.

"The head of security is disabled, madame," the woman

said, looking directly at Evie. "I see you have acquired the infamous Agent G."

"I don't go by that name anymore," I replied.

"I can see why. After all, a world-famous spy has clearly done something wrong," Evie said, going to the man in the bed's clothing and pulling out a Herakles-3 pistol and tossing it to me. She then pocketed a security pass in her dress.

The blonde woman locked the door and began quickly dressing. "The distraction won't last long, and they will notice his absence."

"It doesn't have to last long. It just must last long enough," Evie said, heading to the windows of the bedroom which gave a view of the snowy slopes below. There were lights outside and the sound of snowmobiles mixed with the sound of gunfire that was growing a lot more frantic. "I need you to do a misdirect for at least a little while."

The blonde woman nodded and lifted the man's walkie-talkie. I was certain he was dead now. She then spoke into the walkie talkie in perfect Russian and sounding very much like an older male. Probably the result of a voice replicator. "This is Alexi. I want all forces not presently engaged moved to the South Wall. Secure the brothers and get them to the saferoom. None of the other guests have priority."

If nothing else, that put aside any doubts in my mind that I was dealing with professionals. They certainly had the hardware to pull this off and their deception here would buy them some of the time they needed. Evie clearly had partners on the inside for this and that made me wonder why she needed me— unless it was as a patsy and that wasn't off the table.

"Out this way," Evie said, gestured to the window.

"Alright," I asked, willing to follow her lead for the time being.

The window was sealed from the inside, like a hotel, but Evie proceeded to pull out a ring that emitted a tiny laser torch to cut a circular hole in it. It was straight out of James Bond, and I was someone who was no stranger to oddball gadgets for use in spy work.

"Are you sure you need me for this?" I asked.

"I've killed before Mr. Gordon, but I'm not good at it," Evie explained. "I had someone who was supposed to be here and be my man who pulls the trigger but, unfortunately, he met with a very unfortunate case of the dead. So, I had to improvise. Your arrival at the party and infamous history with lost causes struck me a case of fortune favoring the bold."

"I believe we make our own fortune," I said.

"That is a very male thing to say. We're all subject to the whims of an uncaring world," Evie said, as she finished cutting the hole and forcing the glass out. "Please come with me here."

I reluctantly followed her out on the side of the villa where there was just enough ledge for us to slide ourselves along. The attack on the villa was in full swing now and I wondered what was happening to the guests. I pushed that thought out of my mind, though, as Evie jumped down into the snow a story below and I followed.

We were just outside a doorway with a light still on in front of it. It occurred to me that if the Brothers Assholomov, as Evie had called them, were the kind of people that kept things so close to themselves that if they had a labor camp at the bottom of their vacation spot, then they might be the kind of people to keep something as vitally important as their server rooms nearby as well.

"You're not dressed for this," I muttered, looking at Evie's party dress as I tried to figure out what her next move would be.

"My skin isn't exactly skin," Evie said. "But don't worry, I've never heard any complaints."

Clearly, she assumed I was expecting sex out of this rather than wanting to help for other reasons. Reasons, I admit, that weren't entirely clear to me right now. "How many guards inside?"

"Four," Evie said. "Enhanced Perun Special Operations soldiers. It's a three-room location with the entry hall, computer station, and servers. If you want to back out now, I can't stop you."

"I'm good," I said, shrugging. "In for a penny, in for a pound."

"Pennywise and pound foolish," Evie said, repeating a

less commonly known phrase with pretty much the opposite meaning. "Katya got the late Captain Anatole's biometrics and uploaded them to me to transfer to the keypad. Are you ready?"

"As I'll ever be," I said, checking the gun and chambering a round.

Evie walked up to the door and slid the card in before the door opened. I moved quickly because there was no way—even with the distraction—that this would give me anything more than a few seconds head start. It was utterly insane to go and kill someone—let alone multiple someones—on behalf of someone I'd only met a few minutes before, but perhaps that revealed the nature of my character: I was a machine made to do this.

I rarely pondered the nature of my humanity. For years, I'd thought I was just an amnesiac human and struggled with a desire to find out who I was. The answer, of course, was that I'd been no one. We were made of our experiences and without them, we were someone wholly different. You could never return to the same river and every second we became someone new while not changing what we fundamentally were.

It was a depressing thought as I entered through the door and immediately gunned down a heavy armored cyborg with two shots to the face, spotted a second one before taking him down and ducking behind cover as I spotted a third as he was jumping up from his seat at a computer. I realized that doing these kinds of missions brought a lifetime to me that I otherwise didn't have. I was unable to transcend my nature as a machine made to end lives just as so many other humans were trapped in recursive loops of behavior. Maybe someone, someday, could shake me out of my own recursive loops, but it was more likely I would either die first or degenerate rather than ascend.

The third Perun soldier was shot in the neck and head with three shots before he could bring a KU-123 assault rifle on me. His body fell heavily onto the chair he'd just scrambled up from.

The Perun soldiers were all Borged out with obvious, heavy, and ugly cybernetics that were visible to intimidate onlookers but not as effective as my decade-old machinery that I'd kept maintained. They were the same repackaged tech that had always been, hitting the wall of progress without more money or changes to the laws of physics. After all, the wheel is still being used since its invention at the dawn of humanity.

The fourth and final member of the guard, at least if Evie was correct, should have fallen back and called for backup. Instead, the man made the tactically improper decision of charging out with his rifle. Mind you, it wouldn't have been tactically improper if he'd shot and killed me, but the point of a gun is that it is a *ranged* weapon. You shoot it from a distance. Either way, I managed to plug him twice in the chest before finishing him off with a third shot in the head.

"Are you done?" Evie called from just outside the door frame.

"Yes," I said, dryly. "Four more people cut down in the prime of—"

"Working for a bunch of gangsters, yeah, yeah," Evie said, walking in and heading immediately to the computer terminal with the third guard's body in the chair in front of it. Evie pushed the body out and sat down to work at it. She pulled out an infodrive stick from her hair and inserted it into the side of the computer.

"So, what's really going on?" I asked.

Evie didn't respond for a moment. "I don't know what you mean."

"That's beneath you," I said, crossing my arms, and watching the images flash across the screen that contained a huge number of female headshots and numbers among other, less savory images. "I didn't believe it before but right now, I can confirm that if you're working for the Eastern Alliance, I am the King of Siam."

Evie looked to one of the late soldier's guns near her computer before shaking her head, clearly not liking her chances. "Sacha Chugonov used to run the human trafficking part of their particular branch of the Bratva while his brother was the weapons part. He was every bit the lurid misogynist sex slaver that you'd expect Liam Neeson to kill in a movie. However, despite his reputation as an idiot, he was actually very good at organizing as well as consolidating lesser slavery rings into larger more efficient ones."

"I see," I said. "And this is all—"

Evie interrupted. "I'm uploading a virus to download all of the data for the shape of their kidnapping and smuggling organization plus which brothels are under their control. Better, it's beginning automated day-trading and transfer orders that will empty out their stock portfolio and let the people they've taken be bought back or shut down. I can't help all of them, but I might be able to save a few thousand."

While also enriching herself and ruining the Chugonovs in the process. They might be able to prove fraud but with Sacha's incompetence, it would probably just look like he'd been stealing from the company coffers the same way so many other oligarchs did. I didn't comment on that element, though. "Why not start with this?"

Evie pushed away the gun and turned around to look at me. "I've dealt with a lot of professional killers in my time, Mr. Gordon. Generally, they have rather extreme opinions on sex workers. No, let me amend that, on women in general. They tend to be very sympathetic or very *not* so. The previous guy I'd hired for this role turned out to be not so and had to be dealt with. I wasn't sure which side of the coin you'd land on."

"And now?" I asked.

"I think you'll do something very stupid for a lady," Evie said, softly. "Which is good. It'll make someone very happy someday."

"Sure," I said, not particularly interested. I didn't have any objection to what she was doing—quite the opposite—and mostly believed she was telling the truth. However, it was when a mission was almost finished that they became most dangerous. "I don't suppose you have a way out of here for both of us, do you?"

I took a clip from one of the fallen Perun mercenaries and reloaded my pistol before also sneaking a grenade from one of their belts. It was another sign of the company's inefficacy and poor training that they had grenades in the first place. They weren't exactly useful for guarding a house, servers, or VIPs, but were just another symbol of the mercs trying to appear tough.

"I admit, I didn't plan to take you with me and was going to leave you behind to face the music," Evie confessed. "However, I have a very good reason for taking you to my snowmobile and getting us both out of here."

"A sudden attack of conscience?" I asked, still not entirely comfortable with my back to her.

"Katya's life-monitor just flatlined on my Maelstrom implant," Evie replied, referring to the most cutting edge in infolink tech. "I think our distraction period has just finished."

"I'm sorry," I said.

"I'll honor her sacrifice by getting her sister out," Evie said, standing up and turning off the monitor but leaving the computer running. It was a cheap way of disguising matters, but every extra second would presumably benefit the destruction of Khleb.

"How long until its done?" I asked.

"Eight hours," Evie muttered. "It turns out the processing speed on their servers is shit. I've got the information at least. Destroying Khleb will have to wait. Let's go."

I nodded and followed her out the door, only to find that we were surrounded by six more Perun mercenaries as well as General Vassily. The latter, in simple terms, looked pissed.

"I knew we should never have trusted the robot dogs of Atlas Security," Vassily said. "They sent one of their Living Dolls to destroy us."

"Ever notice they never assume a woman is the mastermind?" Evie asked.

I attempted an old switcheroo by raising my gun in the air as if I was surrendering it. Behind my back, though, was the hand with the grenade.

"Show both hands!" Vassily shouted, clearly not fooled for a second.

Which was, of course, the perfect time to toss the grenade right at Vassily's feet. I'll be honest, I don't remember much of the next several seconds as the explosion was a lot closer than I wanted it to be and shook my cyberbrain around enough that I got the bioroid equivalent of a concussion. However, three of the Perun mercenaries and Vassily were killed instantly. A fourth merc lost his arm and somehow Evie generated some razor like claws from her fingernails to slit the throats of the other two before they could get to their feet.

Evie and I escaped from the lodge easily enough after that, and Sacha, left on his own, didn't discover what had been done to his family's finances until twelve days later, long after the required eight hours. By that time, Khleb had been subject to a hostile takeover by the new Russian Prime Minister's brother-in-law, and they were far more amendable to providing goop for the world than the Chugonov family. It was less altruism than greed as the Chugonovs had been motivated more by spite than pure profit. A chance to see the rest of the world suffer famine and collapse enticed their senses more than billions from food profits.

Either way, Sacha committed suicide by throwing himself out of a window the following year. Well, probably committed suicide by defenestration. It's possible he had help. Evie managed to rescue most of her targets, especially once I helped her hire the right muscle of the "likes sex workers" kind, or at least "willing to do business with them without betrayal." The result was the creation of the Morrigans gang that would not only thrive in America but Eastern Europe, Europe, and parts of Asia too.

And me?

Well, I got to do a little bit more of the kind of work I liked.

However grizzly it was.

CHAPTER FOUR

I finished my story with the final sip of my chem coffee. "There's more to tell but I think you've gotten what you want."

The Cleaver narrowed his eyes. "You killed my father."

He hadn't touched his coffee, which was a shame. It would have made things far simpler.

"Was Vassily your father?" I asked, wondering who exactly was behind the Cleaver's latest shell. It certainly wasn't the original and I was sure that it wasn't Alonzo either.

"Sacha," the Cleaver replied. "You cut him down in his prime. Indirectly at least."

"How old were you when he died?" I asked, leaning back in the booth.

"Fourteen," the Cleaver said, revealing that he wasn't that old. Our world had rapidly gone to shit and been built up just as quickly.

"Then you had no idea what a piece of crap he was," I said, probably making a mistake in taunting the man.

The Cleaver slammed down his vibration blade between us, staring at me with pure hatred in his eyes. "It was my destiny to be the head of Khleb. Do you know what it was like being the bastard of a dead murderer? My mother was hunted down and killed by the families of his victims. I was sold into slavery in a foreign country. I did not climb out of it until the Trikuza let me show them what I was willing to do to escape poverty. You did it *for whores*."

It seemed the Cleaver had inherited his father's prejudices. "Yeah, I did."

"What happened to this Evie woman?" The Cleaver asked,

probably hoping I'd throw her under the bus to save my own skin. Clearly, he hadn't been paying attention to the story.

"It doesn't matter. What's your real name?" I asked, knowing that appeals to logic were pointless here. This was an emotional issue. Still, I wanted to try. I didn't know why I didn't want to kill him. Maybe it was the fact that killing a father, uncle, and son was far too Biblical for my tastes. As rotten as the Chugonov family tree was, I didn't want to be the guy who ripped it out root and stem. Maybe that was stupid of me, but I'd failed to change before. I'd willingly gone back to killing at Evie's instigation, yet it was an addiction that would destroy me. I was married now and wanted to set aside killing for my wife—at least what didn't involve protecting her or those small number of people that I called family.

"Ivan," the Cleaver replied. "Ivan Chugonov."

I raised an eyebrow skeptically.

"Ivan Petrov," the Cleaver corrected. "But Sacha would have married my mother if you hadn't killed him."

I sincerely doubted that. I suspected it would have been more likely for Sacha to kill his girlfriend and possibly the boy before naming them as his heirs. After all, he'd lived through almost the entirety of the boy's childhood with the opportunity to do so with no sign of changing his mind. Still, breaking the image an orphan had of his father was going to be hard. Especially since, well, Ivan here was obviously a psychopath.

"I did my research before I'd come here and while plenty of records had been lost in the Collapse, you're only one of three illegitimate children Sacha Chugunov had. Two of their mothers were killed by Sacha's abuse and one of them had been holding her baby while being burned alive. Maybe your mother was his favorite, maybe it was just he had other people on his mind," I said, taking a moment to stare him straight in the eye, "but I'm not the guy who ruined your chances at being a big shot. You got a raw deal, that's why we're talking, but you don't want to pursue this further." I contemplated what to say next, knowing that this would probably end with fifteen gang members shooting up the place. "There's a reason I told you the rest of that story. I once lionized my father and imagined him to be someone who would be the key to a loving family as well as the secrets of my past."

"And you found out you were a robot," Ivan said, clearly not caring. "You were a machine from the beginning. You never had a family to find."

Ivan had clearly been informed about my true identity from someone with far better resources than a former slave to the Trikuza would likely possess, even one that had managed to work his way up to leg-breaker and throat-slitter. It was probably a man named Snake, but said individual was too smart to have sent Ivan to kill me. No, this was more just a test to let me know Snake was aware of my presence. That he could destroy my makeshift family at any time.

I paused. "Not quite true. I found my family. My real family. It's something you can do too."

My plea was going to fall on deaf ears.

It always was.

Dammit.

"I don't care," Ivan interrupted, shaking his head. "I should have known there would be no answers about my father's death other than some arrogant piece of shit assassin killed him for no reason."

"I don't think you were listening to the story's particulars," I said, disappointed. "Because not dying was a big reason to me."

Ivan sneered. "Not to me. But I'll be honest, it doesn't really matter what you say or what happened so long ago."

"Yeah, I gathered that," I said.

Ivan put down his knife and pressed his fingers against the table before staring at me. "Do you think this is really just about my personal quest for revenge?"

"I was kind of hoping it was," I said, sighing. "Yeah. Unfortunately, you're about to reveal you have powerful friends who want me dead instead."

Ivan's smile broadened. "Yes. People who have paid well for your death, equipped people. People you cannot escape or defeat."

I snorted dismissively. "Let me guess, his name rhymes with Rake."

Ivan's smile vanished. "You mock me."

"Sorry, it's just that you think you're more than a convenience," I said. "The megacorporations, the PMCs, the Emergency Government, the Catholic Church—I'm not sure how I got them on my ass—and the Trikuza are all capable of sending better people to kill me. This is a wakeup call. Nothing more."

Ivan shook his head. "I will not be intimidated. This entire floor is full of explosives. If you don't come with me then I will blow the top twenty floors of this building."

"Which you're in," I replied, surprised at Ivan's ingenuity here. Under better circumstances, he might have put that brain to use for the good of humanity. Then again, under better circumstances I wouldn't have been created to kill for the rich and powerful. Wrong city, wrong people.

"Do you think I'm afraid to die?" Ivan asked. "Especially if it means avenging my father and uncle?"

"People you barely know," I pointed out versus saying that I absolutely believed he was afraid to die and was just bluffing. "Do your men share your view about being willing to die for the ghosts of two dead Russian gangsters?"

"They believe I'm bluffing," Ivan said, confirming no one was buying his claims. "Or they're too stupid to listen in. Either way, you'll be saving a lot of innocent lives if you come with me, Gordon. Think of it as a way of atoning for all the horrible, evil shit you've done. It'll be painful, even more than my father's death, but that is its own way of purifying your soul. I promise I'll run a magnet over your hard drive and put it in a microwave afterwards so they can't bring you back."

"My brain doesn't work that way," I said, dryly. "So, your plan relies on the professional assassin being willing to sacrifice himself for a bunch of strangers? This isn't a movie."

If not for the fact my briefcase contained a device that had spent the past few hours scanning the building for explosives, found the place riddled with them, and was now jamming the signal, I would have taken Ivan to be bluffing too. He wasn't, though. Like the thugs around me, he had given up on life and was ready to go down in the blaze of glory if it meant fulfilling some greater purpose that he'd imagined for himself.

"I believe you want to think you're a human being," Ivan said. "But I'll guess we'll do this the hard way."

He then sent the signal to blow up the Utopian Apartments building, showing I'd grievously underestimated him. I'd call it courageous if not for the fact it was so stupid, petty, and evil. I may have been a bad guy and done some truly reprehensible things, but I had standards, goddammit. Of course, the building didn't blow up. I never would have talked as much trash if it could have.

"Whoops," I said, smiling. "How embarrassing. Don't worry, they have pills for this now."

Seeing that his plan to kill everyone wasn't working, Ivan stood up and was about to say something when the beautiful blonde waitress proceeded to point an explosive-shell shotgun at the side of his head. That was when the combat drones outside, the ones Ivan had prepared to ambush me as part of his attack, took position outside the windows with their machine guns aimed at the thugs he'd recruited instead of me.

"You have no idea who you are messing with, lady," Ivan said, his voice briefly losing its affected grit and sounding much more like the young Russian man he was.

"Neither do you, kid," Kei said, keeping the shotgun right beside his face. "You're embarrassing yourself."

My wife, ladies and gentlemen. The woman Evie correctly predicted I would make happy someday. At least so far, she hadn't killed me.

"You?" Ivan asked, sounding genuinely surprised. "The Runner from Case's file."

"I'm offended I'm a footnote in your file, Case," Kei said, revealing herself.

Yeah, I'd had this all planned. Too bad he didn't drink the drugged coffee. He would have just woke up in a military prison and spent the next ten years cooling off. I had quite a few friends in the US Armed Forces thanks to my long-time association with Atlas.

Tah-Dah!

"Game, set, and match," I said, unfortunately prematurely.

I should have realized Ivan was not someone who was going to come quietly even if he had a gun to his head. He'd already illustrated that he was willing to kill us all to achieve the glory of a "good death" and I should have just shot him then and there. Instead, Ivan remotely activated the EMP mine and proceeded to screw us all over.

Electro Magnetic Pulses don't work like they do in the movies. Once they go off, they destroy any electronics they hit and leave them permanently unusable. Thankfully, the hardware in my body had been hardened against that sort of thing so it just knocked me on my ass and messed with my brain for a few seconds. Everything became a blurry collection of colors like an old television set test pattern and sounded like radio static.

I came too seconds later, only to note that Ivan's hands were gripping my jacket front and was slamming me against the countertop before bashing my head into the side. I could see that the EMP had knocked out the hacked combat drones and a good two-thirds of his own people. The latter poor bastards' cheaper cybernetics had shut down and they were left to die in horrifying paralysis and organ failure.

Kei was the one other cyborg hit by the pulse who didn't get herself disabled and she was up, shooting at the remaining gang members who were only now realizing it was on like *Donkey Kong*. Porn guy got caught in the crossfire while the girl watching *Body Shop* was hiding under her table, having correctly deduced that this was the best place to be as everything went to shit.

The remaining workers pulled their own guns and fired, having been replaced by Kei. This entire thing had been plots and counterplots from the beginning but had ended up degenerating into a Quentin Tarantino movie scene regardless. Oddly, as my head was repeatedly bashed against the counter and my synth-flesh knocked off, I wondered if Tarantino was ever going to get around to that *Hateful Eight* remake set in the Collapse. Dude had to be over a hundred now but was still making movies thanks to 3D-printed organs.

Jamming my elbow with the force of a speeding skycar into Ivan's crotch, I noticed whoever had designed the guy had left on the pain receptors there and he reacted as if someone had destroyed his real genitals. I jammed my fingers into his eyes and felt sparks as the delicate circuitry of both collapsed.

Ivan cried out in pain and took a swing at me that I easily dodged. Much to my surprise, he fled for the door rather than continue the fight. I thought he would have had a backup set of sensors for if and when his eyes were taken out. Mind you, his escape was an embarrassing stumbling affair. Reaching into my jacket, I drew an ER-281 pistol and ended up shooting two of the remaining gang members that tried to cover Ivan's escape.

Noticing that Kei had taken out just about all the remaining gang members, I ran after Ivan. I ended up jumping over the corpse of one of the servers and heading out the door, almost losing my head as Ivan had also pulled out a weapon to cover himself. By the size of the hole it made in the side of the wall beside me, I guessed it was TS7-12 micro-rocket pistol designed to kill bulletproof people like me. He fled down the alleyway I'd originally come from, and I took refuge behind the corner.

"I guess he did have backup sensors," I muttered, guessing he wasn't shooting blind by how close he'd come to hitting me. Ivan just didn't like the feeling of having his crotch and eyes destroyed. It turned out being a cybernetically-enhanced international assassin wasn't nearly as fun as it sounded when you had the possibility of being hurt.

"You won't get out of here alive, Cleaver!" I shouted, taking cover around the corner of the diner. "Maybe we can cut a deal! I'll pay you, right now, a million new dollars to just walk away."

Yeah, at this point I was just trying to distract him.

"I will never dishonor my father that way!" Ivan shouted back.

"You can't dishonor people who don't have honor in the first place!" I snapped back. God, I was sick of this guy.

"I am the Cleaver! I will live forever!"

The shout was accompanied by the sound of a small explosion then silence. Peering around the edge of the corner, I saw Ivan lying dead on top of the body of the dead wino I'd passed on my way here. Paradise was carrying a four-barrel deluxe "Cyber-Killer" handcrafted grenade shotgun that was marked with the words, THIS MACHINE KILLS FASCISTS. I suspected she didn't know it was a quote from Woodie Guthrie but probably agreed with the sentiment regardless.

"Yo, Case," Paradise said, aiming at Ivan's head and blasting it to pieces with a second shot. "I figured you needed some backup."

That was yet another reminder of the steel hiding behind all that hair dye.

I grimaced at the lost data. Still, it was probably a good idea to double tap anyone like him. "Thanks."

"I get a bonus for it?" Paradise asked.

"Tens of thousands," I replied, walking over to the corpse. Kei came out of the diner a second later, a few bullet holes and synth-flesh burns damaging her cybernetics but not actual organs. It would all be easy enough to repair. "What a waste."

"Yeah," Kei said, looking down at Ivan. "I can just tell this man had a bright future ahead of him."

I laughed then shook my head. "Let's go get some real food. My treat."

"Just promise me no more of your war stories," Kei said. "I was there for most of them."

"No promises," I said.

I paid for everyone at the diner massacre to be buried. No one even bothered to investigate once they heard the Trikuza was involved.

LEXICON

AI: Artificial intelligence. Perhaps you've heard of it.

Atlas Security: The world's largest security firm and private army. Atlas Security provides guards, soldiers, weapons, and warfare to the world's governments. It strangely does hold to a standard of trying to end wars rather than inflame them like other war profiteers. As such, it may soon find itself number two.

Arcology: Artificial cities designed to be as close to self-sufficient as possible. The first ones were constructed after the Eruption to replace the formerly largest cities in America.

Big Smokey: The Yellowstone supervolcano that erupted and destroyed Wyoming before covering the Earth in ash.

Big Two Hundred: The world's largest megacorporations that dictate the lives of humanity.

Bioroid: An artificial human being with a cybernetic brain. They are exceptionally rare and only a few thousand exist.

Black Ice: A program created by the Trikuza that seemingly has the power to drive men to acts of violence if not actually control their minds.

Blipvert: A program designed to mind control people into buying things. Shockingly related to Black Ice.

Bot: Non-organic robotic laborers that are usually either mass-controlled by a single Cognition AI or semi-sentient at best. They shoulder the burden of manual labor in the future, creating mass unemployment but allowing the arcologies to exist.

Club Inferno: The hottest club in infospace. The richest and most beautiful avatars in the world gather here to experience all the hottest simulated experiences.

Cognition AI: Unlimited, all-powerful AI that control most of the world's information and finances. May no longer be answering to anyone else but humanity pretends otherwise. Only a dozen or so exist.

Credits: Properly United Nations credits. A Post-Eruption implemented global currency meant to stabilize the economy.

Cyber Dragons: One of the three Trikuza gangs. A former Yakuza clan that has since gone international and become a multi-billion-dollar franchise.

DataSecure: A corporation that provides the best in cyber-security for holding the most precious resource in the Post-Eruption world: information.

Elemental Lords: The lords of the Trikuza. Rich, dangerous, and utterly corrupt.

Emergency Council: The current governing body of the United States. It can overrule most decisions of the previous federal government.

Goop: The mush that you'll never starve on, even if you want to.

Green Foods: The producers of goop and other essential staples of our post-apocalypse cyberpunk world.

The Eruption: The event that destroyed the old world and ushered in the new. It was also, like, twenty years ago so most people lived through it.

Flying Cars: Flying cars. It's in the name.

Frick: A fake swear that Kei's parents tricked her into using instead of the more common f-word.

The Hacker: A mysterious man or woman who uploaded hundreds of terabytes of data detailing the construction of Black Technology to the internet. See *The Leak*.

HOPE: A once-prominent hacktivist group that splintered in the wake of the Eruption.

Icer: Nonlethal ammunition used by security forces as an alternative to just killing people.

Infocom: An uplink to the global infospace system.

Infopad: The replacement for handheld computers and cellphones.

Infospace: The replacement for the internet with vast virtual reality and holographic uplinks.

Invisible Hand: A secret society and club for the super-rich that maintains the hegemony of the Big Two Hundred. May or may not actually exist.

Karma Corp: The largest corporation in the world that manufactures a little of everything but primarily electronics, cars, medical supplies, and weapons. It has recently acquired Green Cereal and Khleb.

Katana: A traditional Japanese sword. Given with a wakizashi to signal the ascension of a Trikuza member to lieutenant status.

Khleb: The Russian version of Green Foods and was the first manufacturer of goop.

The Leak: The information uploaded by the Hacker to the internet. This information advanced humanity's technology close to a century in ten years. It was necessary for survival during the Long Winter.

Lethe: A drug designed to treat PTSD that has since been modified to be a euphoric street drug.

Lightning Tigers: One of the three clans of the Trikuza. They are led by the Lady of Tigers.

Long Winter: A year-long winter triggered by the Eruption. Its disruption of supply lines and crops resulted in dramatic global changes as well as mass death.

Megacorp: Corporations that have been recognized as nation-states in the Post-Eruption world.

The Morrigans: A mostly female gang of sex workers, assassins, and spies that operates out of the Refugee Zone. They eliminated the slavers in the area with the assistance of Case and Lucita.

New Angeles: The Los Angeles arcology that has been effectively rebuilt from the ground up to house tens of millions of new citizens.

Nina: An especially durable high-performance type of bike favored by Riders and street racers. Many of them have unusual modifications like super-jumps and weapons.

Oyabun: The boss of a Yakuza clan. Literally means "foster parent."

RealDream: A system created to simulate full scale auditory, tactile, and visual hallucinations of whatever the programmers want.

RealDream Chair: A chair invented by Barbara Gordon that makes fully-sensed virtual reality immersion in infospace possible.

Refugees: A term for something akin to 10-20% of the American citizenry who were forced to leave their homes due to the Eruption and move to the cities. Many of them were never able to be properly resettled.

Refugee Zone: The temporary shelters for the massive influx of refugees Post-Eruption.

Rider: A new breed of criminal that has emerged in the Post-Eruption era. They are primarily armed couriers and smugglers but also have been known to serve as street mercs and getaway drivers.

Scavs: A derogatory term for refugees due to their habit of living off the old world.

Seattle: One of the cities almost completely evacuated during the Long Winter. It has since been scheduled for reconstruction by the Alders Administration.

Shell: A full-body replacement that leaves only the brain untouched. Shells come in regular human levels and almost indestructible tank-like forms. They are identical in appearance to regular humans.

Simulated Intelligence: An AI with no actual internal will but the ability to perform a wide variety of tasks as well as simulate human interaction.

Steel Phoenixes: One of the three clans of the Trikuza.

Suits: A slang term for corporate executives and workers for the megacorporations. Their loyalty to their company and money is believed to exceed that of any other.

Syndicates: Corporate and criminal alliances that wield vast power in America.

Tanto: A Japanese short sword used by the Trikuza's soldiers to indicate they have been accepted as a soldier.

Techjack: A cybernetically enhanced computer hacker that was modified as a child. Also, a term for a specialized infospace hacker who heavily modify their brains for cybercrime.

Tier 1: AI who are capable of matching human intelligence.

Tier 10: See Cognition AI.

TS80 Maelstrom: An AI-designed cybernetic implant that was implemented in the brains of children. It still is comparable to high-end implants decades later.

Turing Society: A hacktivist offshoot of HOPE that is less involved in information warfare and more playful pranks.

Vertical Lift Off (VLO): A specialized kind of flying car that is capable of landing in or rising from a single spot.

Wakizashi: A Japanese short sword, slightly shorter than a Tanto, used in accompaniment with a katana. Given with a katana to indicate that a Trikuza member has become a lieutenant.

White Triangle: A syndicate of human traffickers, slavers, organ thieves, and black-market cyberneticists.

Yakuza: The Japanese syndicates that have mostly become part of other international organizations.

The Zone: The nickname for the Los Angeles Refugee Zone.

AUTHOR'S NOTE

I'd like to thank you for reading this book. The publishing industry has been changing dramatically since the advent of eBooks. It is now very difficult to get any book noticed, regardless of quality. If you enjoyed this book, you could do some very simple things to help me attract attention.

Word of mouth is the number one source of success for novels, so simply telling family and friends about the book is a great start.

Here are a few other ways of helping, if you are so inclined:

* Post a rating or review on Amazon.com
* Post a rating or review on Goodreads
* Talk about the book or write a review on Facebook
* Tell folks about the book in a blog post.

If you like any of my other books, please feel free to check them out. A lot of my series are interlinked, and you never know when you'll find someone familiar showing up. Case for example is the titular Agent G of the Agent G series that serves as a prequel for this story. Check out those books if you want to learn more about his relationship to the Invisible Hand, the Eruption, the Leak, and Evie Principle.

ABOUT THE AUTHORS

C.T. Phipps is a lifelong student of horror, science fiction, and fantasy. An avid tabletop gamer, he discovered this passion led him to write and turned him into a lifelong geek. He is a regular blogger and also a reviewer at The United Federation of Charles.

BIBLIOGRAPHY

The Rules of Supervillainy (Supervillainy Saga #1)
The Games of Supervillainy (Supervillainy Saga #2)
The Secrets of Supervillainy (Supervillainy Saga #3)
The Kingdom of Supervillany (Supervillainy Saga #4)
The Tournament of Supervillainy (Supervillainy Saga #5)
The Future of Supervillainy (Supervillainy Saga #6)
The Horror of Supervillainy (Supervillainy Saga #7)
Tales of Supervillainy: Cindy's Seven (Supervillainy Saga #8)
The Fall of Supervillainy (Supervillainy Saga #9)

Esoterrorism (Red Room, Vol. 1)
Eldritch Ops (Red Room, Vol. 2)
Agent G: Infiltrator
Cthulhu Armageddon (Cthulhu Armageddon, Vol. 1)
The Tower of Zhaal (Cthulhu Armageddon, Vol. 2)
Lucifer's Star
Straight Outta Fangton
Wraith Knight
I Was a Teenage Weredeer (Bright Falls Mystery Series #1)
A Teenage Weredeer in Michigan (Bright Falls Mystery Series #2
A Nightmare on Elk Street (Bright Falls Mystery Series #3))
Psycho Killers in Love

Michael Suttkus, II, lives in Leesburg, Florida, with three cats, one of which actually likes him, and his family, with whom he fares better. When not working at a game store, he's playing games, reading science books, or otherwise being incredibly nerdy. Also writing! Because he has to feed cats whether they like him or not.

BIBLIOGRAPHY

I Was a Teenage Weredeer (Bright Falls Mystery Series #1)
A Teenage Weredeer in Michigan (Bright Falls Mystery Series #2
A Nightmare on Elk Street (Bright Falls Mystery Series #3))
Lucifer's Star (Lucifer's Star #1)
Lucifer's Nebula (Lucifer's Star #2)
Brightblade (The Morgan Detective Agency, Book 1)
Space Academy Dropouts (The Space Academy Series, Book 1)

Curious about other Crossroad Press books?
Stop by our site:
http://store.crossroadpress.com
We offer quality writing
in digital, audio, and print formats.

www.ingramcontent.com/pod-product-compliance
Lightning Source LLC
Chambersburg PA
CBHW030245200626
46816CB00002BA/518